KAT OF GREEN TENTACLES

Kat Lightfoot is back! Sam Stone's feisty heroine returns in a new Mystery adventure, and this time it's the forces of the dark, and the great Elder Gods that she has to contend with.

When Kat, Pepper and Martin are asked to investigate a girls' finishing school, the obvious answer is for Kat to pose as a teacher. Girls have been disappearing, and the school just feels wrong and oppressive. Before long, Kat is trapped in the cellars, an unknown assailant on her heels … but rescue comes from an unexpected source.

What secret does the strange altar room in the cellars hold? What is making the strange slithering sounds which permeate the house? And who is Edward Brewster and what does he know about the missing girls? It's another mystery for Kat and her friends to solve …

A tale of Lovecraftian horror from the author of *Zombies at Tiffany's*, *Kat on a Hot Tin Airship* and *What's Dead PussyKat*.

KAT OF GREEN TENTACLES

KAT OF GREEN TENTACLES

Sam Stone

First Published in 2015 by Telos Publishing,
5A Church Road, Shortlands, Bromley, Kent BR2 0HP,
United Kingdom.

Kat of Green Tentacles © 2015 Sam Stone

ISBN: 978-1-84583-925-3

USA Edition

Cover Art © Martin Baines
Cover Design: David J Howe

British Library Cataloguing in Publication Data. A catalogue record for this book is available from the British Library.

ACKNOWLEDGEMENTS

With thanks to Charles Martin for originally suggesting the title *Anne of Green Tentacles*, in the early stages of developing the Kat Lightfoot mysteries series, during one of our visits to *The Happiness Patrol* podcast. This went on to become the book you hold in your hands today.

In memory of our much loved, beautiful, intelligent and
funny fur-baby, Jinx, who gave us as much love as we
gave her. So cruelly taken: too young.

Now in kitty heaven.

Keep guarding our driveway, pursuing those little
meeces, and climbing those trees.

You always did chase back the darkness.

RIP Jinx

Prologue

Shirley-Anne was the first girl to arrive back at the school after the summer break: she was early. Even before most of the teachers themselves, who were expected to arrive the following day. Fortunately her father had notified the head teacher, Mrs Lavender, and Shirley-Anne was greeted at the door by the stern housekeeper, Mrs Harris, and led to her room.

Shirley-Anne unravelled her hair braids while she looked at herself in the small vanity mirror on her dresser. Her hair was thick and red and always looked nicer down than tied up, but her mother thought the braids looked 'darling'. Shirley-Anne had an ethereal quality. Green eyes that always appeared to be far away. Pale skin that rarely saw the sun without becoming freckled. But she was by no means plain. Nor was she ordinary in personality. Her friends liked her feisty nature and the slightly tomboyish way she always got herself into trouble. This term, though, she was determined to do better and to make her parents proud.

It had been a good summer. One of the best. And Shirley-Anne was excited to see her friends on the return to Haven Lee School for Young Ladies. Things would be different this year. To begin with, she was on a different floor, one that the senior girls would share when they arrived. Shirley-Anne was excited. As well as having their own rooms and personal privacy, the girls shared a common room. It was a somewhat informal lounge, and it meant they were permitted to invite friends to visit for tea – usually male friends – with permission from the headmistress and a chaperone present of course.

Shirley-Anne was romantic in nature and imagined herself to be sophisticated, a perfect hostess, even as she brushed down the braid-styled waves that indicated she was little more than a girl.

There was a knock on her door and, walking with dignity, Shirley-Anne opened it up to find Mr Sheppard, the butler, and the coach driver holding her trunk.

'Please place it there,' she said, trying to maintain the sophistication she imagined she had, and the two men put the trunk down at the foot of her bed.

After they left, Shirley-Anne went to explore the rest of the floor, opening the doors to the other bedrooms as she went. It pleased her that Mrs Harris had put her in, what Shirley-Anne believed to be, the best room.

The place was clean and aired, and there was no sign at all of dust, nor the usual musty smell that houses have when they have been closed for a few months.

'Shirley-Anne?' Mrs Harris called. 'Supper will be served in the kitchen tonight. Wash up and come down soon.'

'Yes, Mrs Harris,' Shirley-Anne said from the top of the stairs. 'I won't be long.'

Back in her room, Shirley-Anne poured water from the jug into her wash bowl. The water was tepid, but she didn't mind too much. The weather was still warm and it was a relief to wash away the grime from her journey.

Changed and clean, she left her room, closed the door and walked to the top of the stairs.

A strange creaking sound rippled through the floorboards above her head. Shirley-Anne paused.

'Mrs Harris?'

Silence followed: an emptiness of sound that made Shirley-Anne feel more uncomfortable than it should. But then she had never before been at the school when it was this empty. When the other girls were present there was always noise and bustle.

She stepped down onto the staircase, only to hear the next creak, and another. *Definitely coming from above!*

Shirley-Anne had always been curious by nature, and bold, and because she had grown into a young woman recently, though she remained innocently unaware of any dangers that her new maturity might bring, she was sometimes overly confident. She turned and headed for the stairs up to the top level.

The creaking grew worse as she approached. Resorting to her old tomboy ways, she lifted her long skirt and took the steps two at a time.

On the floor above, the strange creaking noise no longer appeared to be there, but was now down, on the floor she had just left.

She hurried back downstairs, cursing herself for falling for what was obviously some silly prank. At least one of the other students *must* have arrived. It was probably one of her friends, playing a joke on her. Perhaps even the kind of joke she would have played herself if she had thought anyone else was there.

She passed by her new room. The door was slightly ajar, as she had left it, but as Shirley-Anne reached the top of the staircase that led down into the hallway, she heard another abnormal sound: a slithering. Something wet.

She had always had a vivid imagination, so she called to mind the thought of a snake sliding across the bare boards in her room.

'Mrs Harris?' she called from the landing.

Mrs Harris didn't answer.

She must be in the kitchen waiting for me, she thought. She took a step downwards. She was afraid. But that was what the culprit wanted, wasn't it? Shirley-Anne straightened her back. The thought of being tricked by another student was worse than the idea of a snake being in her room. Besides, these parts weren't known for snakes, and why would one be upstairs in a closed-up house? It was all so unlikely. Shirley-Anne glared at the door to her room. She wouldn't let them humiliate her. She could run downstairs now and get Mrs Lavender or Mrs Harris, but then she would be the laughing stock all term.

Shirley-Anne took a step towards the door. Then she pushed it fully open. What she saw brought a brief, sharp scream tumbling from her lips.

Then there was nothing but darkness.

Mrs Harris was in the kitchen when she heard Shirley-Anne scream. She ran upstairs, tripping over her long black uniform, which was covered with a white, food-stained apron.

At the top of the landing Shirley-Anne's door was ajar. Mrs Harris hurried forward, opening it wide without knocking.

'Whatever is the matter?' she asked.

The room was empty. Shirley-Anne's trunk stood at the bottom of the bed, still unopened.

'Shirley-Anne? Dinner is ready.'

She heard a peculiar noise behind her. A shuffling sound, like multiple feet scurrying inside the wardrobe.

Mrs Harris noticed that the wardrobe door was closed.

'What are you doing in there?' she asked.

Then, the rustling stopped.

Mrs Harris opened the door, looked inside and saw – *nothing*

1

The cat was a puzzling mix of beige and grey. Not quite tortoiseshell, and not an average mongrel with its long, fluffy fur. I kept catching glimpses of it as the carriage drew closer to my destination. One moment it was on a rooftop, another it was by the side of a road, or peeking out from an alley as the carriage drew to a halt at the crossroads.

I was in Tennessee, Kingsport to be precise, and I was there on a very important mission.

You see, I'm Kat Lightfoot, and I'm a demon slayer; expert, some would say, on the Darkness. An entity that my colleagues, George Pepper and Martin Crewe, and I have come to believe is the source of all evil.

The Darkness first found us in our hometown in New York City, and since then the three of us have been fighting it in many forms. We had come across zombies, nephilims, demons, ghosts and vampires. Now I was preparing for yet another battle. And as always, I was going in with little knowledge of what I would find.

The carriage turned sharply round another corner and I caught a final glimpse of the beautiful cat as it leapt up onto a white picket fence and scurried along the top of it like a circus acrobat walking the tightrope. Then she, and somehow I knew it was a she, leapt down into a garden and disappeared.

I looked down at my hands and then at the carpetbag at my feet and was reassured. My weapons were to hand, and if seeing the cat was any indication, so was something evil. Cats were always patrolling in their attempt to keep back the Darkness. In fact, other than me and my companions, I would say that cats were evil's deadliest enemy – they had saved my hide on more than one occasion!

The carriage pulled up and I looked up once more, to see an imposing building. It was a white mansion or former plantation house in style, with a long pathway from the road leading to a row of five whitewashed steps up to a deep veranda. This was an impressive building and, as confirmed by a bronze plaque on one of the entry pilasters, was Haven Lee School for Young Ladies.

I picked up my carpetbag as the driver clambered down from the front seat and hurried to open the door for me.

'Here you are, Miss Lightfoot,' said Martin Crewe, who was dressed as an ordinary cabbie but was really one of my companions. It was strange to see him in such ordinary clothing. Usually he was dressed, as my mother liked to say, like a gunslinger. That meant he wore leather breeches, and a leather waistcoat over an ordinary men's shirt. He would also invariably be draped in weapons and gadgets. All of which were of his own invention.

'Thank you,' I said, stepping down onto the sidewalk and treating him how I would a normal driver.

Leaving him to wrangle my trunk from the back of

the carriage, which caused me to give an amused smile, I walked up the steps and rang the imposing doorbell.

A bell tinkled deep within the house. Haven Lee had several floors, including a basement. The front door featured beautiful stained glass panels, painted in deep reds and greens.

When the door opened I found myself facing a rather austere-looking woman.

'You must be the new teacher, Miss Lightfoot. I'm Mrs Lavender, the head teacher of this establishment.'

I held out my hand but Mrs Lavender did not take it.

'I don't shake hands,' she said, but no explanation was offered as to why. 'I will send the help to get your trunk up to your room.'

After leaving me for a few moments while she organised this, Mrs Lavender returned, no less stern, and led me through the imposing hallway and into her office, which was through one of a number of the doors to the left.

I closed the door behind me, turned and smiled at the woman who was now sitting primly behind a large oak desk. Her work space was so tidy I could barely imagine it being used at all.

'You're late,' Mrs Lavender said. 'We were expecting you yesterday.'

'I'm sorry. I came as soon as the travel arrangements could be made.'

It had all been rather sudden, but I was fast realising that Mrs Lavender would allow me no slack for that at all. Even though I had done my best to get there quickly, the journey to Kingsport was not an easy one to make from New York. And because I was posing as a new teacher at the school, I had thought it best to travel by the conventional method and not by means of one of

Martin Crewe's inventions. The metallic airship, for example, would have got us there in record time, but would most definitely have been very conspicuous. The most important thing about my role in the school was to avoid arousing suspicion. I had to appear to be like everyone else, even though I was far from ordinary.

Martin had, however, travelled ahead of me, while George Pepper had joined me on the train and coach journey. In the two days that Martin had arrived ahead of us he had managed to procure the coach and don his own disguise, and had rented an old farmhouse for himself and Pepper to stay in on the outskirts of town. Fortunately there was a huge barn for him to stow the airship inside while we didn't need it. But the airship was equipped with everything we might need – including all sorts of weapons that had proved to be effective against the Darkness in the past. It was, as always, our back-up.

Now, I listened carefully as Mrs Lavender went through the list of rules that all staff at Haven Lee had to adhere to.

'No gentlemen callers,' Mrs Lavender said, '*under any circumstances.*' She narrowed her eyes at me.

'Of course,' I said, and smiled sweetly.

After the lecture was over I was shown to my room by another lady. It was on the first floor, and the door to it was the first on the landing near the stairs.

'I'm the housekeeper,' Mrs Harris said. 'And all the teachers' rooms are placed strategically throughout the floors. Since you will be working mostly with the first year students, who are all on this floor, you will have to listen out for any wandering and bad behaviour in the night. Mrs Lavender's room is directly opposite. She keeps an eye on the students on that side.'

'Of course,' I said.

'This is your room,' Mrs Harris said, and she turned the key in the lock. Then handed it to me. 'Your trunk is already inside. Do you need help unpacking?'

'No, thank you. I can manage,' I said, knowing that I didn't want the housekeeper or anyone else to see the stash of weaponry hidden in the bottom of my trunk.

Mrs Harris left me then. It was 6.00 pm, and she informed me that dinner would be served for the teachers and pupils in the main dining room in half an hour.

'I'll be there,' I said.

Mrs Harris frowned then, and appeared to be about to say something else, but turned and walked towards the door instead.

'See that you hurry,' she said, and then she made her way out and down the stairs with barely a sound.

I checked my room and found it to be clean, but sparse. There was a single bed, a dressing table with a wooden stool, a chest of drawers and a door. The door I discovered was that of a built-in wardrobe, and I quickly hung my coat up inside it. Then I pulled out my hat pin and removed my hat. My long hair was tied up in what I hoped would be a prim and proper style for a school governess. Mrs Lavender had given me a stern looking over, but I knew the clothing I was wearing – a brown travel skirt, with a short jacket over a white linen high-necked blouse – was beyond reproach. My trunk contained several similar outfits that would, I hoped, help me appear benign. But what would not be obvious were the men's breeches I wore beneath the skirt, which could be easily removed if I had to respond to any crisis. If such a time came, then I knew I'd be no longer concerned about my cover story being exposed as a lie.

I sat down on the edge of the bed. The mattress was comfortable. At least now I had a few moments to think, before I had to face both students and other teachers.

Some weeks earlier, Pepper had received a communication from a former officer he had made friends with during his time in the army. The war was long over, but Pepper had remained loosely in touch, and then the officer, Colonel Baker, had sent him a disturbing letter.

His daughter, Shirley-Anne, had been attending Haven Lee, and in her senior year, had mysteriously vanished.

Baker told Pepper that an investigation had taken place but no blame could be found, and neither could the 15-year-old Shirley-Anne.

Pepper had made several enquiries about the school, and on learning that another mysterious disappearance had occurred, this time of a young teacher by the name of Mary Cressman, had managed to get the right strings pulled to have me take her place. One disappearance was peculiar. But more than one meant that something strange was happening at Haven Lee, and Pepper, Martin and I had agreed to help Baker find out what. And, if possible, to find Shirley-Anne.

Now here I was, and I found it difficult to believe that this school, seeming so ordinary on the surface, had become a place of concern. I mean, who and what could be behind the disappearances?

A light tap on my door brought me from my thoughts, and I looked at my pocket-watch to discover that half an hour had passed by already. I had made no effort to unpack, and I knew that might look odd. So I quickly opened my trunk, pulled out the first outfit my hands connected with and lay it on the bed.

Then I walked to the door and opened it.

A girl of around 11 years old peered up at me through round-rimmed spectacles.

'Miss Lightfoot?' she said, somewhat timidly.

I nodded.

'I'm Meredith Campbell. Mrs Lavender sent me to lead you to the dining room.'

'Just one moment,' I said.

I picked up the room key from the bed where I had placed it. Then, locking the door behind me, I followed Meredith down the stairs.

The dining room was high ceilinged, with expensive chandeliers. It was clear that Haven Lee had not always been a school, but had once been someone's regal home. The exterior suggested a former mansion of someone wealthy, and the dining room was the most impressive ballroom I had ever seen – and I had been in many over the past few years, not just for socialising, but because balls and parties are notorious hiding-places for the underlings of the Darkness. Vampires feed on victims without being noticed; nephilim seduce young virgins, impregnating them with their evil spawn; and empaths – a recent discovery of ours – are demons that use their power to feed on the extreme emotions found in such places. I didn't expect to find any of these here in the school, but of course, there must be something or someone amongst the staff that was somehow connected. At least, that was our suspicion when we began the investigation.

As Meredith led me to an oblong table that was elevated on a raised platform – an area, I suspected, that had once borne the weight of musicians who played for the dancers below – I soon realised that this was the exclusive seating for the staff of Haven Lee.

'Mrs Lavender,' I nodded, and then the formal introductions were made.

'Everyone, this is Katherine Lightfoot, and she is our new literature teacher,' said Mrs Lavender. Her introduction was formal and cold, and she ignored me from that moment on, staring out with hawk-like eyes at the students seated below the platform. She was a very predatory-looking woman and not at all the sort I would imagine suitable to be in charge of young girls. But then maybe she was exactly right. I wasn't sure, having been educated only at an ordinary New York school and never having had the privilege of attending a finishing school such as this one.

As I sat down in the only empty chair, all of the other teachers took it in turns to introduce themselves.

Sitting at the table were Mr Dupres, the French teacher, Miss Callow, the math teacher, and Mrs Finistra, the dance mistress. There was also a needlepoint mistress, called Mrs Doherty, and a music and art teacher by the name of Mr Kendal.

'It's a delight to make your acquaintance,' said Mr Dupres, who was, I discovered, from New Orleans, and his 'French' somewhat Creole. He also had an annoying habit of constantly stroking and tweaking the points of his moustache, as though he wanted the women at the table to admire it. I've never cared much for facial hair, so I didn't find his moustache in the least bit attractive. I discovered that the dance mistress, Mrs Finistra, was extremely reserved. She sat quietly picking at her plate of food as though it was the worst gruel she had ever tasted, when in truth the chicken soup we were served to start with was delicious, and I ate it with hearty relish.

'Where are you from?' asked Mrs Doherty. 'I'm from Ohio. I don't suppose you've ever been there? It's a small town called …'

I found myself zoning out as Mrs Doherty continued her incessant chatter, following up her questions with comments about herself, which revealed that she didn't really care to hear my answers – a situation that suited me fine, as I didn't want to talk about myself at all. That way, fewer mistakes could be made.

I looked around the dining room as the teachers talked, taking in the pupils. There were around forty girls in total. Two age groups. Juniors and Seniors. Girls between the ages of 11 and 13 were one age group, while the other covered 14- to 16-year-olds. After that age the girls were usually considered 'finished' and sent home to make the expected good marriages that their parents hoped the 'finishing' part of the school would prepare them for. I knew that while at the school the girls were taught refinements and practical skills - being able to balance their household accounts, for example, or to devise interesting menus for their cooks to make – as well as being able to practise their vocal and piano skills so that they could entertain potential husbands.

The girls now sat chatting in subdued tones as they ate the same food that we had been served.

After the soup we were presented with a plate bearing fish and some kind of eggplant salad with pickled artichokes. The fish had been steamed and was perfectly cooked. As our table was served by the butler, whom Mrs Lavender politely referred to as Sheppard, and Mrs Harris, two young maids down below rushed between the tables of girls, rapidly serving the plates from a wheeled trolley.

Dessert was no less appealing, and I now began to

realise why Mrs Finistra was eating so sparingly from each plate she was given: there was an excess of food. I glanced at the girls below, and saw that although they were all slender with the general ease of youth, one or two were carrying excess pounds, and were tucking into the food with excessive relish. I didn't eat the dessert, as although the fruit pavlova looked delicious, I'm not a big eater. Plus, I didn't want to feel too sluggish when I made my planned private exploration of the school later that evening. Also, there's something about being presented with too much food that makes you not want to eat it, and I did feel totally over-faced by the selection.

2

By 10.00 pm the house was in complete silence, and I listened to the tick and groan of the timber settling as the structure cooled. I waited a further hour before slipping from my bed, fully clothed in black breeches and a black shirt, my hair tied back. From the carpetbag I pulled free my gun holster and strapped it around my waist and thigh, then placed inside my Crewe-Remington Sunpan Laser gun, which I had ensured had been powered up during the day. Martin Crewe had designed this gun for me, following his initial prototype. That was way back, when the shop in which we had both worked, Tiffany & Co, had been besieged by zombies.[1] Along with my Perkins-Armley Purse Pistol, this was my weapon of choice. Now I left the Perkins-Armley in my reticule and removed my diamond-shard knife and ankle holster, which I strapped around my right ankle. Then I pulled on my boots to cover it. The boots came up to my knees, but had a special flap in the side that allowed me access to the knife.

Once fully dressed, I retrieved a piece of rope from

---

[1] See *Zombies at Tiffany's.*

the bottom of my trunk. Tying one end around the bedpost, I dangled the other out of the open bedroom window. This was a precautionary measure in case I found myself locked out of the building during my search.

I unlocked the bedroom door, left the room and locked it behind me, stowing the key safely in a concealed pocket in my breeches.

The stairway and landing were silent. But this was a true test of what might occur after dark at Haven Lee School. I glanced further up the staircase to the second floor. As yet I didn't know which of the steps creaked, so I walked lightly up the left-hand side, pausing whenever I thought the wood was about to groan beneath me. Contrary to what people might believe, this is a perfect way to move silently and undetected through a house. The centre of a staircase is always the weakest point and makes the most noise. I had, over the years, learnt to test steps by a minor focusing of my weight on them, before putting my whole weight down. In this way, I skipped two of the steps and reached the top of the staircase without making a sound.

The third floor was easier. Less well travelled than the previous one, these stairs, being near the top of the house also, were still warm. It made the wood slightly more flexible and less noisy. At the top of this floor I saw the door I was looking for. A small entrance that led to the attic.

The door was locked. I retrieved my lock-picking tools and quickly worked the mechanism to spring it open. It did this with a loud click. I paused, listened. The noise had been much louder than I had hoped, and I didn't want one of the teachers who had a room on this floor to come out of their door at that moment. Even wearing black I would have been in plain sight, as the top landing had a huge window opposite the staircase, and light from the full moon was pouring through, illuminating the whole floor.

I could feel my fangs pricking against my lower lip. This always happened when I became excited in some way. It was a natural reaction, and one that had started after my encounter with some amorous vampires.

When I heard no response to the noise, I opened the door as quietly as I could and slipped inside. As the door closed behind me, I was plummeted into complete darkness. I had something with me for that, however. It was a sunpan torch that resembled a jewelled bracelet on my wrist. I twisted one of the jewels and the bracelet lit up. It, like the laser gun, had a small sun panel that collected and stored energy from the sunshine in the day, to be used at night, and it was one of Martin's most ingenious inventions.

Now my arm was lit up so much that the enclosed staircase could have contained a lit gas-lamp. I raised my arm, let the light spread forward and followed it up the steps.

The attic space at the top, as you might imagine, was filled with clutter. Old desks, a musty dressmaker's dummy, several trunks placed in a neat row away from the sloped windows. I turned off the bracelet light and let my eyes adjust to the natural moonlight coming into the room through some dusty and spidery windows. Through one of the windows I saw the airship approaching and knew that Martin must have seen my light. I flashed the bracelet a few times in Morse code fashion to let him know it was me. For obvious reasons, Martin was not firing the engines that night, and he allowed the balloon to drift to a halt above the school roof.

I opened the nearest window and watched as a rope-ladder fell down towards the roof. Martin stabilised the ship and threw me a rope to anchor it. I pulled the rope through the window and secured it by tying a slipknot around one of the attic beams.

Then Pepper climbed down the rope-ladder and, with practised stealth, slipped into the attic through the open window, joining me inside the house.

'Have you learned anything so far?' Pepper asked.

I smiled, showing a little fang. Pepper frowned, but made no comment. Ever since my encounter with the seductive vampires in an old abandoned church in New York, I had been somewhat tainted. If it hadn't been for my cat, Holly, licking and somehow healing the scratch of the vampire, then I might now be one of them.[2]

Pepper too had survived the vampires' scratch, and the awful fate of becoming a gargoyle, when we destroyed the whole coven.

Since then we had strived to find a full cure for me, but my half-turned state remained. One thing I was grateful for was that, so far, I did not have the bloodlust that those dreadful females had. Nor did I have an urge to hunt innocent men or create gargoyles.

Of course none of this had changed the way I felt about the Darkness, or my job to destroy demons in all forms. It was something of a vocation for me, and, I suspected, for Pepper and Martin too.

'I haven't had chance to learn anything yet,' I pointed out as Martin too descended the rope-ladder and joined us. 'But this place makes me nervous. I don't know why.'

Both of the men were wearing clothing similar to

---

[2] See *What's Dead PussyKat.*

mine. This was our stealth wear: black and comfortable attire that enabled us to move silently and in a practical way, and that also helped us to merge with the shadows when needed.

Martin glanced around the attic. 'Well, this looks fairly ordinary.'

'Has anyone mentioned the disappearances?' Pepper asked.

'No. The head teacher is very aloof. Not the sort of person one could befriend and gossip with.'

'What about some of the other teachers?' Martin asked.

'I'm not sure yet. Possibly. I guess I need time to infiltrate them, make them trust me.'

We decided to make a simple search of the school that night.

'Colonel Baker thought Mrs Lavender was hiding something,' Pepper said. 'Obviously the fact that Shirley-Anne has never turned up, nor any obvious suspect, has led the police to abandon their investigation. No evidence, no body, no case.'

I nodded. 'So we begin with Lavender's office. See what we can find out.'

'Good starting point,' Martin agreed.

At that moment we heard a peculiar rustling noise. A thin scraping of what sounded like tiny nails climbing inside the attic walls.

'Rats ...' Martin said.

It was likely. But the sound brought the hairs up on the back of my neck, and the overwhelming urge to go and investigate.

Moving back to the staircase, I pressed my head to the wall and listened. The sound had receded, as though the rats, or whatever they were, had become aware of my presence. That was one of the side effects of my half-turned state, I noticed. Rodents avoided me like the plague. Cats, however, sought me out wherever I went.

Then I recalled the beautiful, long-haired beige and grey cat I had seen on my way there. And I remembered it had had the most stunning amber eyes.

'You okay?' asked Pepper.

I nodded. 'Whatever it was, it's gone now.'

'Then lead the way to Lavender's office and let's check her out,' said Martin.

3

Mrs Lavender's office door was locked, but Martin quickly made light work of the mechanism and we were soon inside. On this side of the building there was no moonlight, partly because there was a lean-to awning over the window of Miss Lavender's office that obscured the light. We didn't want to risk lighting the lamps, however, just in case the glow would be seen by anyone randomly passing the room. I didn't know the routines of the housekeeper or butler yet, and either one of them could be traversing the hallway.

Martin had thought of this problem though, and he retrieved three small items from a pouch hanging from his belt.

'They are torches of a sort,' he explained.

Each of the torches had a small winding mechanism, which Martin demonstrated. As he turned the small key, light began to glow from a tiny crystal at the end of a long, thin tube. There was a quiet ticking sound emanating from the torch.

'A clockwork device?' I said.

'Of sorts,' Martin smiled, but as usual he gave away nothing more, and the truth was, I didn't really need to know how or why his inventions worked, as long as they did and could help us in some way.

The torch was very useful. It gave off a small amount of light that was directional and therefore did not illuminate the entire room.

We began searching the desk and the drawers.

'What are we looking for?' I asked.

'Anything to connect her with Shirley-Anne's disappearance,' said Pepper.

Mrs Lavender's desk was neat. All that sat on the top was a large blotter, a pot of ink in a sealed jar and some fine quills. The top drawer contained a pad of paper and some pencils. The bottom one was completely empty. We quickly moved on and began a thorough search of the room.

At the other side of the room was a cabinet with small drawers. Each drawer had the name of a student on it, or of a staff member.

I turned on my bracelet for more light and rolled the light over the cabinet. It wasn't particularly ornate, but was finely finished with smooth varnished edges. However this piece of furniture had a practical use and wasn't designed to be particularly attractive. I tugged on the first drawer only to discover that it was locked.

'Martin …' I said.

Martin was in the middle of opening a tall cupboard a few feet away from me.

'This thing is locked,' I explained as he came over to me, 'but I can't seem to find any keyhole.'

'Mmm. This is interesting. I haven't seen anything like this before,' he said as he studied the cabinet.

Martin ran his hands over the top and the fronts of the drawers, and probed the sides with his fingers. Then I heard a sharp click.

'What was that?' Pepper asked. He glanced at the door to the hallway nervously.

'Just this,' Martin said, and then he slid open the top drawer of the cabinet. 'There is a secret switch that locks the cabinet. Easy to find once you know where it is.'

Martin pointed out the only ornamental decoration on the cabinet. What looked like a carved wooden lotus flower was, in fact, a hidden lock.

I closed the top drawer without looking inside it.

'What are you doing?' asked Pepper.

'What we need is Shirley-Anne Baker's drawer and the one relating to the missing teacher, Mary Cressman.'

All three of us began to read the names on the drawers, and soon we spotted Shirley-Anne's. I quickly opened the drawer, eager to see what was there. To my chagrin, I discovered it was completely empty.

'Nothing,' I murmured.

We opened Mary Cressman's drawer and found it to be in the same empty state.

After that we searched the other drawers. We found two more that were empty. Names that we had never heard before. One, Julia Maitland. The other, Amanda Pierce.

'These must be former students,' Pepper said. 'But Baker didn't tell me there had been any other missing persons …'

'He probably didn't know,' I said. 'But if these were students, then surely their parents would have made a fuss?'

'More than likely,' Martin said. 'Perhaps they were employees that just left …'

I thought about this for a moment, then suggested that we check the contents of some of the other drawers. We started with the housekeeper, Mrs Harris, who we knew was present at the school. The drawer contained references, information on her previous work history. We learnt that she had been at the school for over five years.

'I guess we can consider that a fairly long term,' I said. 'Particularly as Lavender has been the head here for only six months.'

Martin and Pepper agreed.

Next we opened Mrs Finistra's file.

'She's the music and dance teacher,' I said.

'Says here she was a former student at the school … before the war of course,' Pepper read. 'That means that so far she has the longest history with the place.'

We checked all of the other teachers' drawers, finding various pieces of information. The French teacher, Mr Dupres, had been with the school for only a year. And the needlepoint teacher, Mrs Doherty, had been there for two and a half years.

'Maybe when each of them arrived, that's when one of the others left,' I suggested.

'Or vanished,' Pepper said.

We saw a drawer with my name on it. Inside we found my fake references and equally invented employment history, but nothing more. The last drawer bore the name of Sylvie Valeria. Inside was a pile of paperwork detailing the woman's career and subsequent retirement as the former head teacher of Haven Lee, six months earlier.

'That's interesting,' I observed. 'Lavender keeps all of this information on her predecessor but not on anyone else that has left.'

'Strange,' said Martin. 'I have an idea that we are seeing a pattern here. Let's put it all back, lock up, and go back to the attic. I think Pepper and I need to do some research, and you need to get some sleep before anyone in the house decides to wander about and discover you missing.'

It was a good idea, but we hadn't searched all areas of the house, and I pointed this out to my friends.

'It doesn't matter,' said Pepper. 'Lavender was on Baker's highest suspicion list, and it was she that he wanted investigating particularly. The early bird catches the worm …'

'Meaning?' Martin asked.

'Kat needs to observe the school and get to know members of the teaching staff. Something may well be revealed if we are patient enough.'

'Agreed,' I said. 'I have a feeling about this place. Not sure what it is, but it makes the hairs creep up on the back of my neck.'

'Your instincts are usually right, Kat, so let's follow them and see where they lead us.'

Back in my room, I pulled the rope up from outside the window, untied it from around the bedpost, and stowed it away in my trunk. Then I changed into my nightgown, slipped into the bed and closed my eyes. Somewhere in the distance I heard the firing up of the airship. It sounded like a loud thunderclap, and I hoped that anyone else hearing the noise would think it was just that. Then I slept, and my dreams were full of an amber-eyed cat, that had long beige and grey fur.

4

A loud knock on my door brought me out of my restless sleep. I leapt from the bed, while reaching automatically for the Perkins-Armley that I had hidden under my pillow.

'Who is it?' I asked.

'Miss Lightfoot,' came a young, scared, female voice. 'Hilary is gone!'

Stowing the gun inside a pocket in my robe, which I pulled on over my nightgown, I turned the key in the lock and opened my bedroom door.

Before me stood a girl of around 13. She had long, mousey hair, a freckled face, and round, fear-filled blue eyes.

'Who are you?' I asked, disconcerted that she knew me but I didn't know her.

'I'm Deborah. Deborah Darlington. I'm one of your students.'

'You say someone is missing, Deborah?'

'My roommate, Hilary. I woke up and her bed was empty.'

It was early, around 4.00 am judging by the weak sunlight that came in through the landing windows.

I followed Deborah back to her room. This was of a similar size to mine but had two single beds squeezed in, with a dressing-table between them that the girls shared.

Both beds were empty, but I noticed immediately that one of them, obviously Hilary's, was disarrayed: the covers were not merely pushed back but strewn half off the bed and half on the floor, as though the girl had been tugged from the bed by some tremendous force.

I bent down and looked underneath to check that the girl wasn't just hiding and that this wasn't just a prank to scare her roommate. I still had my bracelet on, so I turned the control jewel halfway and let a narrow beam of light sweep under the bed to prove that no-one was lurking there. Then I turned the bracelet off and looked back towards the door, where Deborah stood. The girl was shaking from head to toe.

'Did you hear anything?' I asked.

Deborah's eyes widened in fear. 'I … thought … there was a snake in the room. There was this sound. So I hid under the covers.'

I stood up, looked over the floor beside the missing girl's bed, and then saw a track of some gooey substance smeared on the rug. I knelt down, sniffed it. There was a vaguely sweet and sickly scent.

'Then what happened?' I prompted Deborah, aware that she had stopped talking.

'Hilary made this noise.'

'What noise?'

'A kind of squeal, but not loud … as though something stopped her before she could scream … There was this scraping noise and then … I was so scared, Miss Lightfoot …'

I looked at the trembling girl and realised how insensitive my questions were. I picked up a blanket from her bed, walked to the door and wrapped it around her shoulders.

'Okay,' I said. 'You're safe now. Let's go and wake up the household. We need to organise a search before it's too late ...'

'Too late for what?' asked Deborah, and then she burst into tears.

'What on earth is going on?' asked Mrs Lavender as she entered the library.

I had placed Deborah at one of the tables, still wrapped in the blanket, and her shivering had eventually stopped. Mrs Harris had placed a tray of tea beside the girl, while Sheppard had been despatched to fetch Mrs Lavender. Now that the head teacher had arrived, I gave her a quick explanation. Then, leaving Deborah in her care, I took Sheppard with me and roused the other teachers.

'We need to organise a search,' I said as they gathered in the hallway. 'Without upsetting the students too much. Hilary Morely is missing and the trail may still be hot.'

'What trail?' asked Mrs Finistra. 'What are you talking about?'

At that moment Mrs Lavender came out of the library and joined us.

'I've left Deborah with Mrs Harris,' she told me. Then, turning to the other teachers, she added, 'Miss Lightfoot is correct. We need to search the house, and we need to be methodical about it.'

We split into three groups. Mr Dupres took charge of one and led them toward the stairs, intending to search the attic and top floor.

'Wait,' said Mrs Lavender. 'The attic is locked, you'll need the key.'

She took a key from the ring she was holding and passed it to Dupres, who left with his group. Then Sheppard led another group off to look at the second floor, while Mrs Lavender and I took the ground floor.

I hadn't been given a tour of the school, so each new room was a revelation, and I couldn't think of a better way to search the house than by legitimately doing so with the headmistress herself.

We searched all of the corners of the expansive library, walked through to the dining room, looked under tables, and opened a huge cupboard that housed the school's porcelain and cutlery. Then we walked through the connecting door to the kitchen. After searching the cupboards, pantry and possible hiding spaces, we came to the door leading down into the cellar.

Mrs Lavender tried the door. It was then that I noticed she was wearing gloves. White gloves.

'She can't be down there,' she said. 'It's locked and no-one ever goes down there.'

'Not even to get the occasional bottle of wine?' I suggested.

Mrs Lavender frowned. 'I don't permit the consumption of alcohol by my employees. But yes, there is a wine cellar down there. Long since emptied ...'

'Well, we should ...' I suggested.

At that moment Sheppard joined us. 'No sign of her upstairs,' he said.

'Sheppard will check the cellar,' Mrs Lavender said. 'We need to go and rouse the girls and start the day off correctly.'

'Mrs Lavender, with all due respect,' I said. 'One of our students is missing and there is no possible way this day is going to start off correctly unless we find her. Now, let's open that door and check down there.'

Mrs Lavender sniffed and handed the set of keys to Sheppard.

'If you insist on going down there, Miss Lightfoot, then I can't stop you. But I don't wish to join you. I'll be in the library when you finish your search.'

I nodded. 'Someone should send for the police, too.'

'I have already organised that,' said Mrs Lavender, and then she turned and walked away.

I watched her leave the kitchen, then turned to the cellar door, taking the keys from Sheppard's nervous fingers.

'Let's do this …'

It took several attempts before I found the correct key. But the lock was rusty and it took a little effort to open. I pulled back the door, and then I noticed that Sheppard was no longer beside me.

'Sheppard?' I said.

He was gone. So I was going down there alone. Probably for the best.

I stepped through the doorway into the complete and enveloping darkness of the cellar, and then my foot caught on something. I stumbled and, without warning, someone behind me gave me an extra push. I found myself tumbling headlong into the gloom, with no way of stopping myself.

5

I woke to find myself at the bottom of the staircase. It was pitch black. I moved slowly. My head hurt and I knew I must have hit it on the way down. Glancing up the steps I could see nothing at all. Someone must have shut the door behind me, which meant that my tumble probably wasn't an accident. I pulled myself up into a sitting position. My head throbbed and I was full of bruises, but fortunately nothing was broken.

I heaved my sore body onto the first, then the second step and, using the wall at the side of the steps for support, attempted to stand. My right ankle twinged, and I gasped in pain. I tested it again. It wasn't broken, but wrenched.

'Damn,' I murmured.

I had a momentary flashback to the fall. The feel of a hand feeding the momentum as I toppled. Someone would pay for this.

I sat back down on the step, then began to shuffle up the stairs on my bottom.

There were 11 steps in all, and when I reached the top I learnt that my suspicion was correct. I tugged and pushed and found that not only was the door closed, but it was also locked. But how? When I had been holding Mrs Lavender's keys in my hand.

The keys … Where were they? *Lying at the bottom of the stairs where I fell?*

I gazed down into the blackness below. Without light the keys were most definitely going to be difficult to find.

Then I remembered my bracelet, and my left hand fell onto my right wrist, seeking and finding the small gem that operated the mechanism. A dull light grew from my arm as I turned the switch. Welcome light filtered into the darkness, filling the cellar with shadows.

I glanced down at the bracelet. The energy pack was almost drained: since using it so much the previous night, I hadn't had time to recharge it. It would take a burst of sunlight to do that, and there wasn't much chance of that reaching me down there.

I hoped that the bracelet had a few minutes' worth of usage left, and that there was enough time for me to shuffle back down the stairs and find the keys.

I raised my arm and pointed the light downwards. The bottom of the staircase was empty, from what I could see, and there was no obvious sign of the keys there.

I hurried down the steps on my bottom, more quickly than I had ascended, as my energy was fast returning and I wanted out of there before the light ran out.

At the bottom I stood once more, testing my weight on the injury. My ankle was sore, but bearable, so I pushed away from the wall and the stairs and, holding out my arm, swept the area around me as I looked for the keys.

They were nowhere to be seen. Which meant only one thing. Not only had I been 'encouraged' to fall down the stairs, but the person responsible had come down after me and taken the keys while I lay unconscious.

What a son of a bitch.

My inner fury was rising and I considered going back up the steps and hammering on the door until someone heard me. But I suspected that the perpetrator would expect me to do that. I raised my arm again. The power pack was almost depleted. I had to find another source of light before it was gone. Surely this cellar had gaslight? Or a window? How else would anyone see down here?

I moved deeper into the cellar, swept the area to the left, then to my right. In each direction there was an open doorway that clearly led off into another room. Then I thought about the layout of the house. There would be a hatch somewhere that fuel would be poured down. If not used now, then certainly in the past. Coal, peat or even wood. All houses like this had them. But which way would it be?

The bracelet blinked as I hobbled to the doorway on the left. Beyond, the light dully illuminated a row of old and dusty wine racks. They were all still full, contrary to what Mrs Lavender had said, of bottles of wine and port. Interesting that she had lied about it. I shrugged. What did it matter? There were many more lies that I was sure to uncover before my stay at Haven Lee ended.

I thought that the wine cellar would be the most unlikely place for the fuel hatch to be, so I turned and hobbled through the doorway on the right. As I crossed the threshold, the bracelet gave a last blink then turned off, returning me to complete darkness.

I rested my hand on the doorframe and limped into the room. Just before the light went out I had seen furniture ahead of me and caught a glimpse of yet another open door. Arms outstretched, I moved into the room – newly blind, I was learning to avoid obstacles.

Then something peculiar occurred.

The only way I can describe this is that it was as though I had been stupidly walking with my eyes closed and now they were open.

The change happened as I pitched forward into an old table that my searching hands had failed to detect. Cursing loudly, I caught myself by gripping the edge of the table seconds before I fell. The sound of my voice echoed around instead of falling flat as it should have done in this low-ceilinged room. And then, the objects ahead of me came clearly into view.

I whistled in surprise as my vision sharpened. It took me a moment to understand what was happening. The fact that I could see again almost brought tears to my eyes as I realised how horrified I had been not really knowing what was in front of me. But the vision was strange. Colourless. Black, white and grey almost. And it was really just the outlines of things I could see, flickering around me.

Then I realised the truth of the situation. I had a new sense. And that sense was somehow activated by sound.

'So, the vampire bite finally proves useful,' I murmured.

The room illuminated, and yet I knew it was getting no brighter; it was just that somehow, whenever I made a sound, that sound carried around the room and reflected back to my vision. Or something like that. Sharper focus is perhaps a better description, but still in black and white tones.

I had heard that bats 'saw' through sound. Something referred to as echo-location. Was this the skill I now had?

I moved deeper into the room, sending quiet hisses

and whistles ahead of me. The vision of the room that reflected in the back of my eyes proved to be true, and it wasn't long before I reached the other side and began to move deeper into the cellar.

In the next room I saw a pile of coal and some stored logs that were drying out for the winter. Haven Lee was fully stocked for any eventuality, and of course this meant that I was also on the right track to getting out of the cellar and finding my way back to the front of the school.

As I walked through the room I noticed that my ankle was no longer hurting, and neither were the bruises I had sustained during the fall. I glanced down at my hands. My fingers glowed and I could almost make out the veins and see the blood pumping underneath my skin.

I found myself beside another door. This one was closed. I glanced up and saw there was a bolt across the top, which I reached up to and pulled back, while tugging the door with my other hand. It didn't budge. I sighed, and the sound carried around me again. Glancing down, I noticed another bolt on the bottom of the door. It was a strange thing to see in a cellar, such security, when nothing from the other side was likely to come through.

Or was it.

I paused halfway through drawing back the bottom bolt. Then pressed my ear against the door.

There was no sound. Not even the scurry of rats on the other side.

As silently as possible I edged the second bolt back, stood up, then pulled the door open. The creak made the darkness explode into light around me.

The room on the other side was mysteriously empty.

No old furniture, no logs, no coal. Nothing.

I walked inside slowly and whistled. The sound rolled around the room and bounced off the empty walls and low ceiling. I tried to work out where this room fell in relation to the school building above. I decided that it was probably still below the dining room, which stretched the entire length of the right side of the house.

I thought about the front of the building, tried to reason out where the fuel hatch would be. It had to be beyond this room, and yet, there was nowhere to go from here. No doors, just walls.

The fall must have disorientated me, I thought. *I should have gone left at the staircase, not right.* I turned then to retrace my steps.

The door was closing behind me. I hurried back, but could not reach it before it slammed shut and I heard the two bolts shoot home with a loud double *thunk*.

6

I was beginning to feel really aggrieved. Not only had I been thrown down into the cellar, and locked in, but the person who had done it was still there and had trapped me once more. This time with no apparent escape.

I considered hammering on the door, but what would be the point? It would only give my captor some perverse satisfaction to think I was afraid or suffering. But fighting the instinct to do just that was a real challenge. I was scared, and furious. Fortunately my mind was used to pushing down my fears and controlling my outbursts of fury: finding yourself in mortal danger on a regular basis teaches you control, if nothing else. I quelled the fear, swallowed the fury, and let it all bubble with silent poison inside me. Someone was going to pay for this, and I knew that person already deserved it. They were undoubtedly behind the missing girls. Perhaps each of those girls had been brought here in the same way I had. The difference between them and me, of course, was that I was armed. And that I was me!

At least, I thought, *I have the Perkins-Armley in the pocket of my robe.*

Remembering the weapon brought me a momentary satisfaction: my enemy would not be expecting an ordinary schoolteacher to be armed. I reached into the robe pocket.

The gun wasn't there.

A few expletives slipped from my lips, the type of blue language that would have made Pepper and Martin raise an eyebrow, but I couldn't help it. How could I have stupidly believed that the person who had pushed me down the stairs, who had then had the sense to retrieve the cellar keys, wouldn't have the presence of mind to search me?

But why would they search me? I wondered. I was supposed to be only a substitute teacher. My references had been faked, but the right people had been paid to verify them. Somehow, though, it appeared that I had been foiled in that way too. Someone here *knew* I wasn't what I appeared to be. But who? And why on earth were they taking young women and girls? What were they doing to them?

I grew tired. The concussion was taking its toll. It passed my mind to wonder if I might even be still lying at the bottom of the stairs, hallucinating this whole experience. After all, it did seem a little far-fetched that I could heal myself and now see almost perfectly in the dark with the aid of some sort of echo-location.

When I stopped making any sound, darkness soon followed. I remained silent, as I didn't need to see right then. I knew the room behind me was empty. So I stayed by the door in case my captor decided to open it and see why I was so quiet, but nothing stirred outside or in.

After maybe an hour had passed by – it was difficult to know exactly – I decided that there was no point continuing to loiter by the door. I whistled again, and the sound bounced around the room. I began to walk the perimeter in order to shake off the fugue that continued to fog my head, and to wake myself up. Thinking hard again about the structure of the house, I realised that this dead end made no sense at all. Fuel was usually stored close to the point of entry into a cellar. It was too heavy to move far. Did this mean that I had completely missed the hatch on the other side of the door, where the coal and logs were?

I shook my head. No. There wasn't one there. I was sure of it.

As I reached the other side of the room I paused, leaning on the wall. My head no longer hurt, but the tiredness persisted. I ran my hand over my hair, which was ruffled and coming out of the long plait I had put it in to keep it neat while I slept. I rested my hand on the wall and felt a breath of air blowing over my fingers.

Air was coming in from outside, as though there were a crack somewhere in the wall. My fingers probed and explored the edges of the bricks. I pressed my face closer to feel the air trickling in. It was stuffy in the small cellar room, but not lacking in oxygen, and this was why. Air was coming in from somewhere. But why couldn't I see the point of entry?

I made that low whistle again, then turned to face the wall as my eyesight returned. I could see movement as the cooler air from outside met the warmer air inside. Yes, there was a crack, or a groove, that was the size and shape of a doorframe: barely visible to the naked eye.

I brushed away the ages-old grime in the furrow around what was obviously a door, then searched for some way to open it.

The door was solid. By that I mean it was made as a part of the wall itself. The kind of door that old houses were sometimes known to have when they had been built with secret tunnels behind the walls. If this was of a similar design then it would stand to reason that there must be a way to open it.

I pushed on the door. It didn't budge. Then I searched the wall spaces either side of it, but found nothing.

That fury and frustration started to bubble up again. My patience was wearing thin. I began to bang on the wall, hammering my fists on it in total frustration until they were bruised and battered.

A few expletives later I was still trapped.

I leaned my back on the brick door and pushed backwards until all the muscles in my body screamed – although my fists were already healing. The whole thing made me feel even more enraged.

I had been turned into some form of half-vampire. I now had rapid healing, and could see in the dark. Why the devil didn't I also get the strength to force my way out of one lousy cellar?

A scraping noise across the other side of the room drew my attention. I could hear the bolts being drawn, and my captor was making no effort to be quiet about it. I shrank back against the furthest wall and cursed my lack of weaponry, but then the wall behind me shifted.

I stepped away as it swung open. A hand reached in and grabbed at my robe, tugging me forward. I whistled, and caught sight of a gentle, male face.

'Come with me if you want to live!' he said. His voice was quiet and had a lilting accent.

I glanced back across the room. The image was

failing, so I hissed a short whistle, and I saw the other door begin to swing open. I wanted to see who was there, but some insane instinct made me trust the stranger. I followed that gut feeling, and allowed him to pull me over the threshold of the brick door.

The stranger slammed the door shut behind us. I hadn't seen who had entered the room, but I had heard something that set my teeth on edge. Snakes. As though the room had been suddenly filled with them.

We were in some kind of tunnel, and a stairway was just ahead, leading upwards and, I hoped, outwards.

The stranger hurried ahead and I followed.

Behind me I heard banging. My captor was now in the very same position I had been and was searching for a way to open the door we had just closed.

'Come on,' said the man.

He was now several steps in front of me. I hurried to catch up, and we reached the top of the staircase in a few more steps. Another door awaited us. Without pause, the stranger pulled a key from his pocket, pushed it in the lock and opened the door. Then he stepped back to let me out.

I glanced nervously down the steps, fearing that our pursuer had been able to do what I had not, and burst through the brick wall to follow us.

'They can't get through,' said the man. 'Only I can open that wall.'

I had assumed that he would be bringing me outside, into the tended and neatly-planted school grounds, but as I passed through the door I discovered that we were emerging into a dense forest.

He closed the door behind us, and as it shut, I saw it fade and vanish before my eyes. I was now looking instead at a trunk of a thick oak tree: a tree that must have been centuries old. I blinked. Maybe my eyesight was failing me again, or maybe that bump on the head really had rattled my brain up. But as I looked around, I realised first that I was actually okay, not suffering some strange mental aberration following the fall, and secondly that we were nowhere near the school and that I had entered a place 'other' than my own world.

7

'Where are we?' I asked.

'Safe,' he said.

'Who are you? How did you ... do that? *Where are we?*' I asked again.

'This is Dalentarth,' he said. 'And I'm Edward Brewster.'

The man calling himself Edward Brewster was a few inches taller than me, with shoulder-length wavy dark hair. His chin was covered in a few days' beard growth, as though he had been trying to grow it, or else had been unable to find the opportunity to shave. He had a slightly dishevelled appearance, which made me realise that the latter was probably more likely. But his eyes, a warm green in colour, glowed with good humour and friendship, and I knew that my instinct to follow him had been right.

It was daylight in the forest, and I looked around at the lush greenery. It appeared to be the middle of summer in Dalentarth ... but in Kingsport it had been the beginning of autumn. But then, I was no longer in Kingsport: I was somewhere else completely. And this place had a magical quality.

'How did you know I was down there?' I asked. 'And how did you do *that*?'

'It's a little difficult to explain,' he said.

I noticed again there was a slight lilt in his voice, as though English wasn't his first language. When he spoke he put a beautiful, musical curve around the words.

'Oaks make great doorways,' he said. 'And I'm always tuned into the new land. Especially when there are movements from the *other* world.'

He was speaking in riddles, but the idea that oak trees made good doors had a kind of bizarre, but logical, sense.

'That's why humans use them to make doors,' Edward continued. 'They are always trying to pass through. A subconscious thing, you might say. But they don't really know how to *open* them. They don't know the ways of my people.'

'Who are your people?' I asked.

Edward merely smiled.

'Come, I'll take you back home now.'

I walked back to the oak.

'Oh no, you don't want to go back through that one,' Edward warned. 'You remember … there's something waiting there …'

I frowned, but followed him as he set off through the trees.

The forest held that type of silent beauty that undisturbed nature has. It was so still that I began to wonder where the wildlife was. There were no birds singing in the trees and no insects buzzing annoyingly around us.

Edward led me deeper into the woods. This confirmed my instinctive knowledge that we were far from the school. How that was even possible I didn't know, but it would have been rude to keep questioning him: the man had done something incredible and had saved me from some unknown fate. Had he not done so, I would probably have ended up as a missing person's statistic myself. Though I still had to get back and contact Pepper and Martin to let them know what had happened, or that might yet be the case.

'Not far now,' said Edward.

We came upon a long, narrow river that flowed through the heart of the forest.

'This is beautiful,' I said as I watched a shoal of koi carp leap out of the stream, fighting their way upriver against the natural flow. It proved that nature was at work here despite the silence.

We continued walking, and eventually emerged from the trees.

'What is that …?' I asked.

In the distance something miraculous loomed on the horizon.

It was rock, but a glowing rock that appeared to grow out of the land itself. The shape was city-like. As the sun fell directly on it, the stone lit up, sparkling and gleaming like a precious gem. To all intents and purposes it could have been a luminous crystal city.

'You must try to forget what you have seen,' Edward said.

'That *is* a city, right?'

Edward nodded, and I noticed then the strange curve of his ear poking out through the strands of his long hair. It was pointed at the top. I glanced away, trying not to be indecorous. It was not my place to study the man, or to judge him, but something jogged in my mind, a childhood memory of fairytales involving pixies and fairies. Weren't they supposed to be small? Almost invisible to the eye?

Edward began to follow the line of trees in the opposite direction from the city. I looked back at it once more, wishing I could go closer, see it in all of its glory.

'Not all of my people are as welcoming as I,' said Edward. 'It is dangerous for one of your type to remain long in the Old Kingdom. Please see this as merely a passage you have traversed from one place to another.'

I wondered what exactly he meant by 'one of your type', but said nothing as I followed him. What was my type exactly? Was he seeing me as human? Or could he sense that something else was part of my make-up?

We came upon a rickety old bridge that crossed over the flowing river to another bank.

'Now I must leave you,' Edward said.

'But … where do I go?'

'The bridge is a doorway to where you need to be. All you need to do is cross it.'

I placed a hand on the rail. The wood appeared rotten and pitted, but somehow I trusted that it would support my weight. I wasn't naturally gullible, but I did completely believe in Edward Brewster – though I didn't understand why. I took one step onto the bridge, and then another.

'Thank you. You have …' I said, looking back over my shoulder.

Edward was gone.

I scanned the trees behind me, the river, downstream and upstream. There was no sign of him at all.

I shrugged, then continued my progress across the bridge. Beneath, the river flowed, while behind me, the forest remained quiet. I picked up my pace.

As I reached the other side I was assaulted by the sounds of nature, as though I had suddenly removed a pair of earplugs. Crickets chirruped in the fields around me. A frog plunged into the river from the bank. Somewhere I heard a cow lowing, and birds chittered in the trees along the riverbank.

I stepped off the bridge and immediately turned to look back the way I had come. Across the bridge, in place of the forest, there was now a meadow. Curious, I remounted the bridge, as a murder of crows flew squawking overhead. From the middle I peered at the meadow but could see no change. The forest was definitely gone, and I was certain there was no way for me to return to it. None of the doorways would work without the magic Edward used to activate them – whatever that might be.

I glanced downstream, looking for that beautiful city, but there was no sign of it at all.

Back over the bridge, the way that Edward had suggested, there was an open field ahead, where long grass grew, and I thought I saw the bushy tail of a beige and grey cat. It looked just like the one I had noticed near Haven Lee School when I had first arrived there.

I began to make my way across the field, determined to follow the cat. Cats were always around, lurking somewhere to help, and they had never let me down yet.

'*Kat?*'

I turned to find a surprised Martin Crewe standing nearby. He had a fishing rod in one hand and a pail full of fish in the other.

'Where on earth did you come from?' he asked. 'And why are you dressed like that?'

8

'Dalentarth,' Martin explained, 'is a magical forest found in the Faelands. It's also mythical.'

'Mythical?' I said. 'I was there.'

'I don't doubt it,' said Martin.

'He talked of the Old Kingdom …'

'The Faelands *is* the Old Kingdom,' Martin explained. 'And I think, from his description, your rescuer, Edward, must be one of the Fae. You see, mythology says that there are two types of Fae, the light and the dark. Which one is your Edward, do you think?'

'I don't know, but dark implies *evil* doesn't it? So I would say he must be light, because I felt no wickedness in him.'

'That's not really so in the case of the Fae, though I understand that misconception,' Martin explained. 'If memory serves me, the Seelie were the first and original Fae. Then there are the Unseelie, the Dark Court.'

'Unseelie?' I said. 'Seelie are Fae, Unseelie must be other?'

'That would be logical to assume. But I must admit I don't know much about them, so I will research it and let you know more.'

'Okay,' I said. 'But it may not matter, and probably has no bearing on the case we are investigating. Still, I'm curious about Edward and how he knew where I was, and that I needed help. He was very vague on it.'

Pepper had been silent as he bustled around the kitchen. We were in the farmhouse Martin had rented, which was just across the field from the bridge – Edward Brewster had somehow known to bring me there. After I had appeared in the field, Pepper and Martin had studied the bridge. They had quickly established that, however I had got across it from Dalentarth, it appeared to only work one way. Crossing back the other way had just taken them to the other side of the river. No forests or cities in sight. Now, Pepper placed a hot drink down in front of me.

'What is it?'

'Tea,' he said.

I sipped the tea and tasted the sickly sweetness of sugar. 'I don't take sugar …' I complained.

'For shock,' said Pepper.

I wasn't in shock, but it would have been rude to say so when he was obviously concerned.

'Let me check out this head injury,' Martin said.

'What head injury?' I asked.

'There's blood, in your hair at the back of your head. You must have taken a nasty knock.'

'Oh!'

I let him look. He ran his fingers through my tangled hair for a moment. 'That's weird. There's nothing there,' he said.

I had yet to tell them both of my newfound ability to heal, or of my use of echo-location to see. And so, I explained the full extent of my experience, while both of my friends remained quiet.

'Well, we thought that there might be side effects associated with your condition,' Pepper said. 'Better that they be beneficial, rather than negative ones.'

'Like craving for blood you mean?' I said.

'Yes. You aren't craving blood, are you?'

'No. But I really would rather have my tea without sugar.'

Pepper retrieved my cup, tipped it down the large kitchen sink, then poured me another one without complaint. This time without sugar. Then he placed it back on the table before me.

'So what do we do?' I asked. 'Obviously someone working at the school is involved with the disappearances.'

'Yes. You didn't see who though?'

'Sheppard was there, then he left. The only people who knew I wanted to search the cellar were him and Mrs Lavender. So, logic says one or the other or both of them is involved. And I wouldn't be surprised about Lavender, as she is a cold fish to say the least. She's also unwilling to shake hands, for some reason.'

'That is weird. But hardly evidence of corruption. In a situation like this we could legitimately bring in the authorities to shut the school down pending an investigation. The only problem is, how do we explain your escape and appearance here?' said Martin.

'I could say I don't recall what happened due to the head injury?'

'Yes – but now you have no injury,' Pepper pointed out.

I had to admit that would make my story unbelievable to the authorities. I sipped my tea and thought for a moment.

'I need to sneak back into the house,' I said.

'How?' said Martin at the same moment that Pepper said, 'No.'

'That's not a good idea,' Pepper continued.

'It's the only option. And it will make our enemies wonder how I did it, and perhaps make another move to rid themselves of me.'

'Which is precisely why you aren't going back there,' Pepper said.

'I don't know how we could sneak you back in unobserved at this stage either,' Martin added. 'Especially since you didn't find a legitimate way out of the cellar.'

'She's not going back in there,' Pepper said again. 'Aren't either of you listening to me?'

'I am going back, Pepper. And you're going to help me. We'll leave the blood in my hair, and you, a concerned gentleman, are going to lead me right back up the steps, with a confused memory of what happened.'

'But we've already said that won't wash with the police. They'll want a doctor to check your wound,' protested Martin.

'True,' I said. 'But do you really think Lavender is even going to call in the authorities? I'll hazard a guess that this is going to be swept right under the rug. Missing child and injured teacher on the same day notwithstanding.'

Pepper and Martin glanced at each other.

'It could work,' Martin said.

'I don't like it. We know that there is real danger there for Kat,' Pepper said.

'I'm willing to take the risk. I've faced worse.'

'Yes – but usually we are beside you most of the time,' Pepper pointed out. 'I mean, we couldn't hear you cry for help from here, could we?'

'Well, no,' said Martin. 'But I do have a way that we can keep in touch. We would have to remain nearer to the school, as the machine works only at a short distance.

'What machine?' I asked.

'I haven't named it yet.'

'What does it do?' I asked.

'Well, it directs static electric pulses into the air. These can then be translated back into the original sounds by the receiver.'

'You're speaking a foreign language again,' Pepper pointed out as we both stared blankly at Martin. 'What are static electric pulses?

'Well. You know that little shock you sometimes get when you touch something metal, or another person?'

Pepper and I both nodded.

'I was initially trying to make some form of portable telegraph machine. But then I realised how uneconomical it would be to spend time miniaturising something that was already available. Plus it takes so long to tap out a message in Morse code. Then I recalled the works of Thales of Miletus, and the research of William Gilbert in the 17th Century.'

To illustrate his point, Martin walked over to the fur rug in the middle of the floor. He rubbed his feet on it for a few seconds, then he reached out to Pepper and a spark flew from him, giving Pepper a minor jolt. Pepper pulled his hand away.

'You've just felt a minor electrical shock. I'm sure you've experienced that before. That is static electricity.'

'Yes, of course,' said Pepper. 'But how can you create this energy in this small device?'

'By extrapolating from Thales' original experiment with a piece of amber, which is inserted inside the device. Instead of being rubbed against fur, it picks up the static from the body of the user. As you carry the device around with you, so you are effectively charging it. The mechanism inside then converts the energy. As you speak through it, it becomes sound. And that sound carries to a specific receiver.

Martin explained a little more, but as usual it was way over my head and I was certain that Pepper understood him even less.

'We can talk to each other through it?' I said, making him get to the point.

'Yes. You will carry the receiver, and we can communicate through it. So if you needed us, you could call for help into it.'

'A communicator. Let's call it a … a statcom …' I suggested.

'I like it,' said Martin.

As Pepper drove the carriage into town, Martin explained to me how to use the statcom. It was a small, round device that looked exactly like a pocket-watch.

'Good design, it will be inconspicuous,' I said.

'I always try to disguise our equipment,' Martin said. 'Anyway, you open the device like this …'

He pressed a button on the top of the watch and the frontage flicked open, just as any pocket-watch would have done. Inside I could see the mechanism: again, anyone looking at the device would just have seen the moving clockwork and assumed it was what it appeared to be, and nothing more.

'This is the clever bit. You turn the winder anticlockwise. That activates the mechanism and begins to send the pulses out to my receiver. And just in the back … there, see? That's the amber.'

As Martin turned the apparatus, the back of the watch opened. Inside I saw thin metal gauze over a glowing gem, which I recognised as amber.

'Press down the release switch at the top of the device. Then, talk here,' Martin said.

I took the apparatus from him and did as directed. 'Hello. This is Kat.'

At the same time, Martin picked up a similar device. This one was attached to a larger machine by a long, thin wire and was hidden in a carpetbag by his feet. As I spoke, I could hear my voice coming through Martin's receiver.

'Received loud and clear,' Martin said, and his voice came through my own receiver. 'All seems to be working. As soon as you're back inside the school and are alone, call me and check in.'

'I will.' I closed the device and placed it in my pocket just as Pepper brought the carriage into the kerb right outside the school.

9

A surprised Mrs Harris opened the door to Pepper's insistent pulling of the bell. The housekeeper was flustered but seemed genuinely pleased to see me as I stumbled into the hallway and, crying, fell into her arms.

'Miss Lightfoot! What on earth! We've been looking everywhere for you.'

'I found this poor lady wandering the streets. She seems to have hit her head. The bleeding has stopped, I checked. I'm a physician, you see,' Pepper lied. 'She was able to tell me she worked here, but not how she came to be outside, so dishevelled. I thought it best, in order to avoid scandal, that I brought her straight here and not to the authorities.'

At that moment Mrs Lavender came from the dining room and into the hallway.

'Thank you, sir,' she said. 'That was most considerate of you. Can we rely on your continued discretion?'

'Of course!' Pepper said.

He gave her a card with a fake name on it. He and Martin carried several fake identities around with them, as did I when needed.

'Should you need any further assistance I'm staying at

the nearby hotel,' Pepper added.

'The Willoughby Regent?' Mrs Lavender said.

'Yes, dear lady,' he answered.

'Thank you,' said Mrs Lavender, taking the card. 'Now, if you would excuse us, we must get Miss Lightfoot back to bed. It has obviously been a most trying experience! Mrs Harris …?'

Mrs Harris began to lead me to the staircase and back up to my room.

'Thank you. You've been my rescuer,' I said to Pepper, still playing the maiden in distress.

I then let Mrs Harris take me upstairs.

My room appeared undisturbed. My bed covers were still thrown aside from when I had leapt out of bed at the call of the student who had come to report the missing Hilary. My absence had been so short that Mrs Lavender – if indeed she was behind it all – had not had time to erase signs of me from the school.

I let Mrs Harris put me to bed, but as soon as she left the room I was up and searching through my carpetbag and trunk, ensuring that my weapons were still there. All were untouched. But I mourned the loss of my Perkins-Armley, which had been taken by my assailant.

Once I had checked the weapons, I changed my clothing. My nightgown was torn and dirty from the fall into the cellar. I poured tepid water into the washbowl on the dresser, washed my hands and face and sponged the blood from my hair.

I slipped on my breeches, then a day skirt over the top. Inside my clothing I stowed an array of weapons, placing the knife back inside my boot. I wasn't going to be caught short again.

Then I remembered that I was supposed to check in with Martin. I opened the pocket-watch, turned the mechanism and spoke into it.

'Here. All okay. Haven't spoken to Lavender yet. Will check in again in an hour or so.'

'Good. Speak soon,' came Martin's voice.

I stowed the device down into my blouse, pushing it firmly and safely down the front of my corset. If I was incapacitated again, I was hoping that my assailant wouldn't search further than my pockets, and if he/she did, they might consider the device nothing more than a harmless watch.

There was a sharp knock at the door at that moment. I opened it to find Mrs Harris holding a tray of food.

'I thought you might need breakfast,' she said.

'It's still morning?' I was surprised. It felt to me that a whole day had already passed, and yet of course it had been only a few hours.

'Yes. All the girls are in the dining room with the other teachers,' Mrs Harris said.

'Thank you, but I think I ought to go down and join them,' I said.

'But. Your injuries …?'

'I'm feeling much better. And I do have to teach today,' I said. 'Have they found Hilary?'

'Who?' said Mrs Harris.

'The girl that went missing. The one we were searching for?'

'No-one is missing. Only you went missing, Miss Lightfoot,' said Mrs Harris.

'Oh!' I murmured. So we were going to play that game, were we? No missing girl, only a teacher with a head injury saying there was one. I decided to play along.

'I really must have been imagining it. I had some kind of fall. I hit my head. It's all so confused!'

'Of course it is, dear!'

'Still. I ought to start earning my salary,' I said.

Then I bustled past the woman and made my way downstairs and into the dining room.

Mrs Lavender did not look up as I entered, but all of the other teachers that I had met the night before stared at me as though I had giant warts growing out of my nose.

The students were unnaturally quiet. I looked around for the girl who had reported her roommate missing. What was her name? Somehow I couldn't recall it. Maybe I wasn't quite healed from my head injury after all? Be that as it may, there was no sign of her.

I walked through the silent pupils and made my way up onto the platform, then took my seat beside Mr Dupres as I had the previous night.

'Good morning,' he stuttered.

As they all mumbled a polite acknowledgment of my presence I began to wonder. Were they *all* in on it? Or was it I who was wrong? Doubt of my own memories began to creep in. It was a peculiar feeling, as though my mind were being submerged in icy water. I felt numb. Cold. And I questioned everything that I thought I knew or believed in.

Had I imagined Hilary's disappearance? Had I imagined being in the cellar? Had I imagined Edward Brewster? If so, then how had I found my way to Pepper and Martin? How did I remember it all so vividly?

10

My first teaching day went as well as could be expected. I won't say that I did anything more than a reasonably good job. I wasn't a teacher really, but I did have good English skills, and I was well-read, so I gave the students a sort of writing test. It was the best thing to do to keep them all interested and busy and to give myself time to think.

'Write a story about something that frightens you,' I said.

The girls, 13 in all, stared at me for a moment, then quietly picked up their quills and began to write. While they wrote I watched them. They ranged between the ages of 11 and 13 and they were all, supposedly, from good families. Families that cared about them. Were any of them aware of the other disappearances? Or were they ignorant of what was really happening in the school while they slept?

The morning dragged. I knew that nothing more would happen until the night-time. But I had to keep up the pretence, even though my real job was to find the culprit and save the rest of these young women from whatever fate had befallen the others.

At lunchtime we went through the motions of eating.

Again excessive amounts of food were placed on the pupils' and teachers' plates. The students were encouraged to eat everything by Sheppard and Harris as they patrolled the tables.

My appetite wasn't there, however, and I just pushed my food around the plate, just as the dance teacher Mrs Finistra did.

'Outside time,' called Mrs Lavender, and the girls stood up like automata and pushed their chairs under the table.

'You are on the duty roster to watch them outside with Mr Dupres,' Mrs Lavender told me. 'However, as this is your first day, and in view of your injury ...'

'I'm happy to do it. Best to keep busy,' I said.

Mr Dupres stood up, pushing his chair under his seat in the same, almost mechanical manner that the students had. I stood, mimicking him, as I decided it might be best to appear as though I was fitting in, then I followed him off the stage and outside.

We went through the large patio windows that lined the wall of one side of the dining room.

As we stepped over the threshold, the fresh air hit me, and it was a relief. I had not realised how stifled I had felt inside.

Mr Dupres sighed.

'You'll get used to this place and its ways. They may seem odd at first, but schools need discipline and routine, even if it is a little more rigid here than usual.'

'I suppose so ...' I said. 'But what is it with Mrs Lavender? She's so ...'

'Distant?'

'Yes. That's an apt description,' I said.

'I understand her a little,' Dupres explained. 'There was a time, when she first arrived, when the families of some of our students objected to her regime. They had wanted some other teacher to take over, a relative of one of the wealthiest families as I recall, but the school board chose Mrs Lavender because of her excellent references. She's had a tough time, had lots to prove, and still the families aren't happy with her.'

'Not surprising,' I said. 'I heard that some students had just vanished from the school ...'

Dupres laughed then. 'Oh, that's a rumour they like to spin. No-one has "vanished" – anyone who has been here one day and gone the next has been removed by their parents as a protest, or is a runaway. Girls of this age group can be very rebellious. Fortunately, there is always a waiting list for Haven Lee. It has a fine reputation as a finishing school.'

I was about to point out to Dupres that I knew a student had vanished the night before, but then I realised that actually I didn't know that. I had never met Hilary. I didn't know for certain that she had not been removed from the school by her parents. But that didn't explain Baker's missing daughter, Shirley-Anne, did it?

Of course, I couldn't disclose my knowledge of her to Dupres without revealing that I wasn't who I claimed to be. Nevertheless, his view on the situation did give me a different avenue that we could pursue.

Being outside of the school seemed to have a freeing effect on the students too, and on Dupres, who was far more talkative than I had expected he would be. The girls were running around the yard, playing. Some of them had skipping ropes, others were playing tag. All of them appeared to be happy and normal. Far different from their overly quiet, subdued attitude inside.

Half an hour later, Mrs Harris came outside and shook a large handheld bell. As it rang, the girls grew quiet once more and walked back to the open doors, falling into four lines.

'Your class is on the end,' said Dupres. 'Seniors this afternoon. I'm teaching French to the group you had this morning.'

'Thanks,' I said.

'It's a short session though,' said Durpres. 'An hour, then afternoon break. After that the whole school goes to choir practice.'

I nodded and thanked him again. Then I led my students, now completely silent, back inside.

11

Dinner was a long, drawn out affair that evening, as if the teachers did not want to retire. After the students were dismissed to their common room, Mrs Lavender and the teaching staff all withdrew to the drawing room, which was off the library.

Evenings were the only time when the girls were not fully supervised by the teachers. However, among the senior students there were a number of prefects, who had monitoring duties and patrolled the corridors, taking their positions very seriously.

I went with the other teachers into the drawing room for a while, though all I wanted to do was be alone. It had been a very long, and very trying, day all in.

'A little port, Miss Lightfoot?' Mr Dupres offered.

So, Mrs Lavender *did* permit a little after-dinner port.

I refused the offered glass, and glanced around as the other teachers took one. I wondered if the bottle was one taken from the considerably stocked cellar below, and reasoned this was more than likely. Why Mrs Lavender had told me she didn't permit alcohol of any sort in the school, and then clearly did, was another mystery.

As everyone settled down – each had his or her own specific chair and routine – I waited to be barraged with the questions that I had been expecting them to ask all day. But no-one did. The whole incident was clearly being brushed under the carpet – though I did catch Mrs Finistra giving me the occasional curious look, and Mrs Doherty did not prattle on as she had the evening before; in fact she was unusually quiet once she had her glass of port.

The atmosphere in the drawing room was most peculiar. The teachers hardly spoke to each other, and I observed that they all appeared to be somewhat drowsy.

'Well, I think I'll turn in,' I said, excusing myself to the group.

No-one answered me. Not even Mr Dupres, who had fallen asleep in his corner chair with a pipe gripped between his teeth. I slipped unobserved through the door to the library and made my way through the house, back to my room.

Locking the door behind me, I retrieved the statcom and contacted Martin, then I filled him in on the rest of the day. Especially on Dupres' view of what really happened to the students who mysteriously vanished from the school.

'Make some enquiries about Hilary ...' I said. 'And check out some of those other names we saw on the filing drawers. If it turns out that those students were just moved to other schools, then it would shed a different light on things. It wouldn't explain Shirley-Anne's disappearance though.'

Martin left me with a promise that he and Pepper would do some research the next day.

'Always have the device on you,' he reminded me. 'We are only a short distance away and would be there as soon as you needed us.'

'I will,' I said. 'I'll check in again in the morning.'

'No midnight excursions,' Pepper's voice said through the device.

'No. I'm trying to appear benign. Even though someone here already knows that I'm not.'

I turned the device off, then removed my day clothing, but left my breeches and shirt on, so that I was ready for action if I needed to be. Then, I turned the oil lighting down until it was almost dark, but not completely so.

I lay on the bed. I wasn't afraid of complete darkness, but it was more convenient to have some light in the room, even though I could now use a different form of 'seeing' by way of my echo-location. Even so, the small amount of light gave me some comfort. I was exhausted, but I lay with my eyes closed, going over the events of the day, trying to make sense of it all.

Then, without realising it, I drifted off to sleep. I dreamt of a beautiful magical forest and a crystal kingdom where fairies danced in a magnificent ballroom. The ballroom looked just like the dining room at Haven Lee.

Morning came, and the routine of the school day fell into place. I got up, washed, dressed, took on the role of the teacher, which was a little challenging, even for me.

I fell into a schedule of working, eating, sleeping. This went on for a few more days without incident. Every evening I observed the same ritual performed by the other teachers. They all partook of the port and became sleepy, and at that moment I always took my leave of them.

It was as if I was waiting for another incident to happen. I had lost the desire to look around the school. I merely went wherever I was supposed to, and when I wasn't on duty, or eating the meals with the others, I went back to my room and sat quietly reading from books I borrowed from the school library.

On the Friday, at the end of the teaching week, Mrs Finistra came to see me in my classroom. The students were in choir practice again, and I was sitting down to attempt marking the stories I had set them earlier in the week.

'A weekend to ourselves,' Mrs Finistra said. 'What are your plans, Miss Lightfoot? I'm going home to see my husband and children.'

It hadn't occurred to me that the dance mistress had another life.

'Really?' I said. 'Where do you live? I always thought you just boarded here, as I do.'

'I do during the week. My home is in the next town, and it's too far to travel in every day. But Harry will collect me tonight and have me back Sunday night. It's not much of a rest; I have washing and cleaning to catch up on ... But I get to eat the food I like. I mean, the school food just tastes ... a little odd, don't you think?'

I thought this an unusual thing to say, since the food tasted perfectly fine to me, though there was always too much of it.

'I'm too far from home,' I said. 'I'll be staying here.'

'All alone, then? At least Sheppard and Harris will be here. And the students of course. Mrs Lavender has plans herself this weekend, I believe, otherwise she's usually around. I know it's not easy when you're trying to make a good impression, but don't spend the whole weekend marking. A walk in the local park would be good for you.'

I marvelled at the sudden friendliness of the teacher,

as she had barely spoken to me all week. But I nodded and said I would try to get out for some air. As it was, I planned to have a proper meeting with Pepper and Martin to see if they had learnt anything from their research into the missing students. Other than checking in morning and evening, I had been unable to have a proper discussion with the men, and I hadn't really been able to leave the school at all, because of one duty or another.

As Mrs Finistra left my classroom, I turned over the page of the story I had started to read. There I saw a graphic drawing. The student in question had drawn a picture of what she was most afraid of. It looked like a giant octopus bursting out of a cupboard.

I started to read the story again. One passage jumped out at me within the text.

'There's a monster that crawls through the walls,' it read. 'It took my friend, Hilary. Mrs Lavender said I imagined it. But you know it's true, don't you, Miss Lightfoot?'

I flicked back to the top of the page and the name of the student: it was Deborah Darlington. And then I remembered the girl clearly. And where she sat in my classroom. Deborah was quiet and rarely drew attention to herself, but how, when I had been actively looking for her, had I forgotten her name and her face?

I folded the story and pushed it down into my corset alongside the statcom device. Then I flicked through the other stories to see if any of the other students had made any reference to a monster in the walls. None had. So I left the pile of papers on the desk and went in search of Deborah.

Now that I remembered her, I also recalled the room that she had shared with Hilary. It was on the opposite landing from mine, in the far corner.

All of the girls were still in choir practice, and I thought it was probably a good idea to check Deborah's room while she was absent.

I opened the door, looked inside and grew instantly annoyed with myself. I recognised the room, but had somehow forgotten all about it until I had read Deborah's message. Why had I done that?

The two beds were made up now, as though a new occupant had been moved in to share with Deborah. I hadn't noticed any new faces in class – though this was hardly a surprise, as I was only just getting to know each of the girls by name.

I entered the room, closing the door behind me in case any of the teachers passed and wondered what I was doing. I wasn't terribly sure myself what I was looking for.

The room had the same type of built-in wardrobe that mine did. I opened it, glancing in at the clothing hanging from the rail. Hilary's absence was glaringly obvious: the wardrobe was empty on one side.

I thought about Deborah's drawing of the octopus tentacles coming out of the half-open closet door. It was a very competent drawing for an average 13-year-old girl. Clear and direct. The girl had some talent, and probably a big imagination too.

I stepped into the cupboard. It was big enough for me to stand to my full height inside, and wasn't as shallow as it had first appeared. It was double the depth of an average wardrobe in fact. I examined the interior, which was lined with dark wood. Probably oak. I tapped along the back wall and the panels gave a flat thud, which indicated that thick wall was behind them: just as expected. Other than the wardrobe's size, there was nothing unusual at all about it.

I climbed out and closed the door. Then I looked around Deborah's room, under the bed, in the drawers, but all I found were the girl's personal effects. There were no more drawings and no more stories.

I supposed that the best thing to do would be to wait for her and then talk to her about the picture and about Hilary, but at that moment I heard voices approaching. I hurried back to the wardrobe, climbed inside and pulled the door partly closed, so that I could see outside while hiding behind Deborah's clothing.

Mrs Lavender entered the room and bustled inside, glancing around.

'Put that down there,' she said.

I then caught sight of Sheppard and another man, who was dressed in a coach driver's uniform, and noticed that they were carrying a large trunk between them. They placed it at the bottom of the missing Hilary's bed. Then they left.

Mrs Lavender glanced around the room once more, then she hurried out, closing the door behind her.

I waited a moment. Then, just as I was about to come out of the closet, Mrs Harris came in with a girl of around 12 years old.

'This is your room, Charlotte. Your roommate is called Deborah. She's a nice girl and I'm sure she'll take care of you.'

'Thank you, Mrs Harris,' Charlotte said.

'Leave your coat here and I'll take you downstairs to choir practice. The school has a wonderful choir; we all sing in the Brethren Chapel on Sunday too. It's a nice church, run by the Reverend Philip Airley and his wife.'

'I'm Catholic, Mrs Harris,' Charlotte said.

'Oh, that doesn't matter, as long as we all worship a

God. Come along now.'

Charlotte placed her coat over her trunk and followed Mrs Harris outside.

I leaned against the back of the wardrobe and sighed. Then, as I pushed away, the wooden panel behind me moved. I turned around. A small opening was now visible in the rear of the wardrobe. I ran my fingers over the ridge, then pressed against it. The panel slid aside with barely a creak and the wall behind it opened up.

12

I had found a secret passageway. It was dark inside and I wasn't sure that I wanted to go wandering around in there alone, so I paused at the doorway. I hadn't used the echo-location vision since my incarceration in the cellar, and was a little concerned that I might simply have imagined the new ability, so I pulled the wardrobe door fully closed behind me, blocking out the little bit of light from the bedroom, and gave a low whistle. The back of the wardrobe, and the doorway beyond, lit up for me with that peculiar black, white and grey outline vision that seemed to pulse ever so slightly with the sound waves that echoed around .

I couldn't think why I had been doubting myself so much. I had been so confident and so secure in my abilities when I had explained them to Pepper and Martin, but since my return to Haven Lee, I had begun to believe that I had imagined the whole thing. Even having been down the cellar. And I had been fighting a sense of lethargy that was stopping me from further investigation. Until, that was, I had seen Deborah's picture and story and it had jogged the memory back into the forefront of my mind. The realisation that it had been pushed back, or even suppressed somehow, was worrying. It rocked my confidence still more.

My logical brain considered this feeling but couldn't explain it. I was not by nature easily scared. After all that I had faced with Pepper and Martin over the last few years, to be scared of one dark passageway was irrational. But there was no denying that my heart was thumping hard in my chest. It was a sensation I would normally put down to adrenaline, and would quite enjoy as a rule. Now though, I was almost overwhelmed with terror. It was unreasonable. Insane. Above all, I didn't feel in control of my mental and physical faculties. This wasn't me.

Cold, damp air wafted in through the hole in the wall. I stepped toward the threshold and glanced inside, sending another low whistle out to light my way.

I could see ahead of me, and there was a long passage. Nothing obvious to be afraid of, and my echo-location ability reassured me that I wouldn't be plummeted into endless darkness.

I forced my frozen body to move and crossed the threshold, giving another barely audible whistle to keep the air flowing with sound so that my echo-location receptors, wherever they may be, would continue to give me the sense of sight. The last thing I wanted was to find myself coming across something I hadn't seen, but fortunately even the quietest whistle sent sound out far enough ahead that I could pick up my pace without fear of stumbling.

Now I was out of the cupboard and into the passage that overwhelming phobia I had experienced receded considerably. I started to feel my usual strong and confident self again. My mind cleared, and I became aware of the fact that some form of heavy fugue had previously clouded my thoughts, and my memories. I halted for a second while those memories reasserted themselves, and it occurred to me that this week, as I had begun to go through the motions of being a teacher at the school, I had actually started to believe in my fake identity. I had fallen into the same kind of benign pattern and routine that all the other teachers had. Now, though, I could see that they, and the students, acted out this pattern day in, day out, with little reprieve. The difference in the students between when they were inside the building and when they were out of it was marked. It was as though, outside, they felt the same relief that I was now experiencing, a return to normality when free of the structure – the institution of academic life, perhaps – and permitted to be children again in the yard.

I pushed my mind back to the present, sent another whistle out, and began to walk again.

The passage went on for quite a way. Then I saw another panel in the wall. I paused to examine it. Thinking of the layout of the house, I realised that this must lead to another of the girls' rooms on the first floor. Perhaps another wardrobe had a similar, hidden panel inside.

Seeing no obvious way to open the panel, I walked on. Then I began to notice that other identical panels were placed at intervals along the way. Did every room, even mine, have one of them? In which case, it didn't really matter whether I locked my door or not. Whoever knew about these passages could probably get into any room in the house.

That put Lavender even more firmly into the suspect category as far as I was concerned. She was the one person who had access to all areas of the school. She had also known I was going into the cellar, and clearly hadn't wanted to go in there herself. And her manner was even more distant now than it had been when I had first arrived at the school. All odd behaviour by anyone's standards. I also recalled that she had never once broached the subject of my return to the school with Pepper. Or of how I had injured my head. And she certainly had not asked me how I had managed to escape from the cellar – but then, if she had done, that would have meant her acknowledging that I had been down there, wouldn't it? And that Hilary was still missing. All of which she didn't want to discuss or admit. But where did that leave the other teachers? Because surely none of them had made any attempt to speak of it either.

I weighed up each of the teachers at the school and found them all lacking. Even Mr Dupres and Mrs Finistra, who were the only two that ever bothered to talk to me at all. But then, what about me? I began to analyse my own behaviour over the last few days. Why, for example, hadn't I taken Sheppard aside and spoken to him about the incident? It seemed that while in the house itself, I had no motivation to do so. Now, all I wanted to do was tackle the man head on.

There was something very wrong inside the house, and whatever it was did not affect these hidden tunnels.

I reached the end of the long passageway and paused. To my left was evidence of another doorway back into the school, to my right was an open doorway and beyond that a staircase leading upwards. I made a decision and turned towards the staircase. Taking the steps two at a time, I was soon on the second floor.

Perhaps these were old servants' stairs? After all, I had wondered about the origin of the house when I had first arrived. It was not a structure purpose-built as a school, but rather a former mansion converted into one.

I wondered who had originally owned the house, and how they had come to lose it. All questions that would seem perfectly appropriate to ask of the staff, or even of Mrs Lavender. But I thought it would be safer if I put the problem to Martin and Pepper instead.

I found on the next floor a passageway of a similar layout to the one below. This passage ended, however, with a staircase downwards, that I soon discovered led all the way to the ground floor, ending perhaps somewhere off the kitchen.

At the foot of the staircase I located another semi-hidden door, and on close inspection found an opening mechanism in the form of a lever by the side. There had been no such device beside any of the other doors I had seen, and so, unsure if I could find my way back to Deborah's room by retracing my steps anyway, I pulled the lever.

The door opened with barely a scrape of brick on the flagstone floor, and I found myself in the pantry. As I stepped through, the door closed automatically behind me.

I listened at the pantry door. No sound came from the kitchen, but now that I had left the passageway and entered the main building again, my mind began to fill with a dampening fog. I tried to focus on the thoughts that had occurred to me in the passageway, but found it difficult. The only thought I could hold onto beyond remembering the passageway itself was that I needed to speak to Sheppard.

'Oh, hello there, miss,' said Sheppard, entering the kitchen as I closed the pantry door. Almost on cue.

'Ah, Sheppard.' I said. 'I wanted to talk to you. That morning …'

Sheppard began to flush to the roots of his greying hair, and I felt my confidence shrink as my heartbeat increased with panic once more. Even so, I held onto my recently regained memory of his possible involvement.

'Someone pushed me down into the cellar. Then they locked the door. I don't suppose you know who that was, do you?'

'Good grief, miss!' said Sheppard. 'I'm sure I don't know what you mean!'

'Yes, you do,' I said. 'And I'm going to get to the bottom of it.'

The fog receded still more as I spoke. My mind was clearing itself from whatever was affecting it. I could see that Sheppard was unnerved, afraid. Perhaps he was even feeling that same awful panic that I had.

'Sheppard, I want to know what you know.'

'I don't know anything, miss. Really I don't.'

I looked into his terrified eyes and believed him. His mind was as fuggy as mine had been, but he had no ability to push back the fear and help himself as I had. There would be no point in pushing the question now, as I believed that he would just go further into his terror. I decided to bide my time once more, and somehow get to talk to him again when we were both outside the building.

'We'll talk again,' I said.

I turned and walked out of the kitchen and into the hallway.

It was time that I tackled some other things head on instead.

I went to the room where the girls had their choir practice with Mr Kendal. I could hear the piano playing all down the hallway, and young voices raised as though they could sing high enough to reach heaven. I had to speak to Deborah Darlington, and I would take her out of choir practice and into the yard if I had to.

I didn't knock on the door, I just walked directly in. Mr Kendal was playing flamboyantly, and the girls were lined up before him in order of height, with the smallest of them at the front, as though they were already in the church in front of the congregation.

None of them acknowledged my presence. Then it occurred to me that the song they were singing was rather strange.

'Ancient God, spirit of old,
'Send my soul to R'lyeh,
'Elder God, bringer of death,
'Come forth from thy wounded tomb,
'Seeker of the greatest good,
'Eater of the purest,
'Treat mankind as you should,
'Bring about unrest.'

'Mr Kendal?' I said.

Kendal carried on playing, and strange words continued to pour from the lips of the girls. Each of them sang as though they were the most beautiful, profound and angelic words.

'Stop!' I said loudly.

But the singing went on and on until eventually the awful panic surged once more inside me and I turned and ran from the room.

13

'From what you say,' said Martin, 'there is some kind of influence asserting itself on the building.'

Martin and Pepper had been expecting me when I entered the hotel where they were staying. I had called ahead to them on the statcom, and now I sat with them in the hotel's dining room. I had a glass of wine in my hand and a plate of chicken and vegetables before me.

'Yes. I feel different again now that I am away from there. But inside, it is difficult to hold onto myself. My memories become confused or suppressed, and the longer I am there, the worse the feeling gets.'

'And now that your mind is clear?' Pepper asked.

'I think Lavender could be connected, but I don't know how. She hasn't really done anything to convince me of her guilt. She is just very distant. And all of the teachers are like that. Even I, to be honest. Because the thing in the house is making us like that. Then there is Kendal. He was teaching those girls that awful song. I didn't understand it at all, but the words and tone terrified me. From outside, it sounded like choir music, but once I entered the room, it became harsh and violent. As though it was some form of chant rather than a psalm. Like an incantation.'

'Your instincts are probably right,' Martin said. 'Though I have never heard of this R'lyeh place, I shall do some research on it.'

'Good. What have you found out about the missing pupils and teachers?' I asked.

Pepper and Martin exchanged a look.

'Some of them did leave,' said Pepper. 'I went to see the parents of a girl named Josephine Boulogne. They said she had been very unhappy there, so they had removed her. When I pushed to know why she had been unhappy, they refused to explain. Then, this morning, I received a note from Josephine herself. She said she would meet with us. Perhaps you should be there too.'

'We didn't manage to locate any of the missing teachers, though,' Martin added.

'When are you meeting Josephine?' I asked.

'Tomorrow morning,' Pepper said.

'Okay. I'll be there.'

'Perhaps you should stay here tonight, too,' Pepper suggested. 'I'm not comfortable with the idea of you going back to the school until we know more.'

Away from the school, the thought of return shouldn't have concerned me: I was my usual fearless self. But then, when I remembered the strange behaviour of the girls and the music of Mr Kendal, a genuine terror rose up in a flood of irrational emotion. The prospect of staying at the hotel, even for one night, really appealed to me.

'I'm quite drained,' I said. 'Perhaps I will go back and collect some things and then return here for the night.'

'Good,' said Pepper. 'You can have my room and I'll share with Martin tonight.'

With that settled, I was able to eat my meal, and I recalled that it was the first full meal I had consumed in days.

'The food is odd at the school,' I mentioned as the waiter cleared away our plates.

'In what way?' asked Martin.

'I feel over-faced by it. They pile the plates up rather too much, but it also tastes … wrong. I thought it was fine until Mrs Finistra mentioned it too. Now, away from there, I know it's not right.'

'Does anyone else seem to notice?' asked Pepper.

'The students all eat it. As do the teachers, except for Mrs Finistra. There's this emphasis on having empty plates at the end of every meal too. I thought it a little peculiar then, but more so now.'

'That influence again,' Martin suggested. 'It's dulling some senses, but enhancing others. The fear factor for example.'

'Yes. Exactly,' I said.

After dinner, Pepper walked back with me to the school. Then he waited down the street while I went inside, collected my carpetbag and placed inside it my toiletries and a change of clothing.

As I came downstairs, Mrs Lavender was hanging up her coat on the coat-stand by the front door.

'Miss Lightfoot, could I have a word with you, please?' she said.

'I'm just on my way out. Perhaps we could talk tomorrow?' I suggested.

'No. It is important.'

'Very well.'

I followed her into her office and found myself sitting once more in the chair opposite her as we looked at each other over her impressive desk.

'Mr Sheppard has told me something very disturbing today. He says that you mentioned the cellar incident to him. Now, I've given you the benefit of the doubt, Miss Lightfoot, but really we cannot have our teachers behaving so disgracefully.'

'What on earth are you talking about? Someone pushed me down the stairs and locked me inside. Since when is that me behaving disgracefully?'

'Pushed you down the stairs? What nonsense! You were down there drinking. It is perfectly obvious that you have some kind of ... problem. Which is why I told you we did not permit ...'

'Problem? A *drink* problem? Why would you think something like that?'

'Well, I was warned about you,' Mrs Lavender said.

'Warned? By *whom*?'

'One of your referees came back with a warning about your ... appetite for wine.'

'I have no appetite for wine. I merely drink it on social occasions like everyone else. Surely you've noticed that I don't even touch the nightly ration of port that you give out in the drawing room.'

Mrs Lavender frowned. 'I have noticed, but I thought ... that you were secretive about your needs.'

'Mrs Lavender, who told you this? I can't imagine any of my referees would.'

'I'm afraid that is confidential,' Mrs Lavender said. 'But I can see that we have had some kind of misunderstanding.'

'So this is why you've never asked me about what happened on my first morning here. You thought I had gone into the cellar and raided the wine. Good heavens! Someone locked me in there. Then they herded me into another locked room.'

Mrs Lavender's eyes widened with genuine fear. 'Who?'

'I don't know. But only you and Sheppard knew I was down there.'

'No. Everyone knew. I told the teachers as we were

gathered in the library, set to look for Hilary. Then we received a message from her parents, telling us that she had found her way home. The girl had run away, can you believe?'

'Hilary is *safe* then?' I said.

'Of course. And she will be back in a week's time. We've suspended her as a punishment. Didn't any of the teachers tell you?'

'No. In fact they've mostly avoided me this week. I guess that's because they think I'm some kind of sot.'

'I'm so sorry, Miss Lightfoot. We seem to have misjudged you. But I am most concerned about this cellar incident nonetheless. Why would anyone lock you in?'

'And push me down the steps to begin with,' I reminded her.

Mrs Lavender's frown deepened. 'You know, ever since I took over here we have been plagued by occurrences of the foulest kind,' she confided. 'I have adopted a distant manner because I do not know what to do about it. If I were to bring in the authorities to investigate, then it would bring scandal to the school. Scandal that could cost me my job. I have many enemies who would like to see a change of management. But, if someone has been injured, and lives are being put in jeopardy, then I must surely act.'

'Yes. You must. But I'm okay, and nothing more has happened since. So, perhaps it is best that we keep this conversation between ourselves for now.'

'Of course. But wouldn't you rather I put the record of your ... habits ... straight with the other teaching staff?'
'Not for now,' I said.

'But why?'

'Because it is probably one of them that did this to me. If they believe that you aren't suspicious of the incident, then you aren't any threat to them, and probably neither am I. But if they learn that you now know what really happened, that changes everything. Doesn't it?'

'Good lord, I hadn't considered that,' said Mrs Lavender.

'I know. So let's keep this conversation between the two of us, for now.'

'Very well,' said Mrs Lavender.

'I won't be here this evening. I'm staying with friends. But I will be back sometime tomorrow afternoon,' I said.

'Thank you for telling me. We wouldn't want to assume that you had … vanished,' said Mrs Lavender.

'Indeed,' I answered. 'But I would like to talk more with you about the disappearances.'

'Oh, they are mostly just girls being girls. Going home to their parents because they have argued with their roommate, as is the case with Hilary and Deborah. Or parents deciding that another school would be better for their little darling,' she explained.

'But that isn't always the case, is it?' I said.

Mrs Lavender bowed her head for a moment. 'We'll talk more, as you say. But not now. I fear we may be overheard.'

She glanced sideways at the huge stationary storage cupboard near the door. I looked at it, making a connection with the wardrobes in the bedrooms that hid doorways into the passageways I had found.

I made no further comment, but Mrs Lavender's actions had revealed that she too knew about the corridors behind the walls. And she suspected that someone else did also. Our brief connection did change how I felt about her. I now believed that she was not a part of the sinister happenings in the school.

14

Martin, Pepper and I had a nightcap in the bar of the Willoughby Regent Hotel while I recounted my conversation with Mrs Lavender.

'You most certainly should get her outside and have a more detailed conversation,' Martin said.

'Call me cynical,' Pepper interrupted, 'but if I were guilty of doing something, I would throw the blame elsewhere. Perhaps Lavender is lying to you.'

'I had considered it a possibility. But she wasn't lying. She was genuinely afraid. It doesn't mean that she doesn't know something about what's happened though. Or that, by not acting, she hasn't become a quiet accomplice.'

'True,' Martin said.

'It's been a long day,' I said. 'I think I ought to retire.'

'Of course,' said Pepper.

I had already taken my bag to Pepper's room, and had the room key in my pocket, so I said goodnight and went up the stairs to the second floor.

As I reached the room I discovered that the door was closed but unlocked. I thought back to my previous visit and couldn't remember locking the door again behind me when we left the room. I cursed myself for my carelessness, then opened the door, entering the room. The lamplight was on low, and the bed turned down. Unlike earlier.

It made me feel a little better that it hadn't been I that had left the door open, but rather the maid service that had come into the room.

I closed the door behind me, locked it and pushed across the security bolt at the top as well.

Then I quickly undressed, washed and slipped under the covers.

The pillow smelt of Pepper's musk perfume, as did the sheets. I closed my eyes and tried not to think back to our 'almost' marriage, which now felt like a lifetime ago, even though it was little more than six months since the vampires in the church had changed my life forever.

I heard two men talking loudly, and drunkenly, outside on the landing, but their raucous, laughing voices soon passed by. But for a sliver of light coming in under the door, the room was dark, cool and quiet. I closed my eyes tighter and looked for sleep, but it was difficult to find. I was still somewhat apprehensive and my mind was working overtime on all of the things that had occurred since I had arrived at Haven Lee. It was as though all of the suppressed thoughts could now be processed and my mind wouldn't let me sleep until I had thought every detail through. But what was I looking for?

Drifting off to sleep, I thought I heard a quiet hissing and slithering sound, and my dreams were full of snakes and the sea.

Daylight leaked into the room around the edges of the curtains, and I awoke to the noise of movement outside. I reached for my pocket-watch on the bedside table. It was

7.30 am.

Throwing back the covers, I sat up. I had promised to meet my colleagues for breakfast at 8.00 am, so I rubbed the sleep from my eyes and hurriedly made my ablutions.

I didn't recall falling asleep, but knew that exhaustion had finally taken me in the early hours. Glancing in the mirror, I noted the dark rings around my eyes, the paleness of my skin, and as I finished dressing, I pinched my cheeks for good measure to bring some colour into them.

In the hotel restaurant, Pepper and Martin had already found a table near the window. I hoped that they wouldn't notice my tired state as I joined them.

Pepper was on his feet quickly to hold my chair as he always did. Martin being Martin, he never offered. His mind was elsewhere, in a world of inventions most likely, and it didn't bother me at all, as I was perfectly capable of pulling out my own chair. However, propriety in public was always observed among us. We tried, though often didn't succeed, to bring as little attention to ourselves as possible.

'Bad night?' asked Pepper after the waiter had left with our order.

'Is it that obvious?'

'Not really,' said Martin. 'You just don't seem to have your usual vitality.'

It was true, I wasn't feeling great, and hadn't been since I had arrived at Haven Lee.

'I did some more research on your Fae encounter,' Martin said.

'Yes? What did you learn?'

'Not much that I could consider to be fact, but mythologically speaking, I now understand what the two courts are. We thought that the Unseelie were the opposite of the Seelie ...'

'Yes,' I nodded.

'Well, it seems that there is more to it than that. They are like the poor relations. You see, one of the Fae Kings decided to create his own Song of Making. A recipe for creation, you might say ... He wanted to create more Fae, but the result was not what he had hoped for.'

'What happened?' asked Pepper.

'The Unseelie Fae happened. They were magical but somewhat monstrous, from all reports. The Kingdom rejected them, imprisoning them in their own court, and they were never permitted to interact with the Seelie Fae.'

'How awful. They weren't responsible for their own creation, so why should they suffer?' I said.

I didn't have much time to ponder this, however, because at that moment someone interesting entered the dining room.

She was a young woman of maybe 18, and I perhaps wouldn't have noticed her except for the fact that Martin leapt from his seat in an uncharacteristic display of gentlemanly behaviour. Even Pepper, who was always observant, didn't have time to react before Martin.

She approached our table with a swagger of bustle. Her fashion was expensive. The latest Parisian designs that all the young and wealthy women were going for. Something I myself was less concerned with. Her skirt and jacket were in a pale green silk, and she wore a white, low cut blouse that accentuated the slight heave of her full bosom. She had soft blonde hair, pulled up high on her head but draping down behind her, falling over her shoulder, and her presence caused a stir in the dining room. There was a ripple of contagious energy that she brought with her. It made me feel, almost, like myself. As though her vitality could be passed to anyone who needed it.

Martin bowed over her hand. By then, Pepper was also standing. He bowed to her from the opposite side of the table, and then Martin made the introductions.

'Josephine Boulogne,' he said.

'How kind of you to recognise me,' Josephine said. She had a trace of a French accent.

'I saw your portrait in the parlour at your parents' home when we called to see you,' Martin explained.

'The picture doesn't do you justice,' Pepper said.

'How sweet of you,' Josephine smiled at both of the men. It was not the type of shy smile I would have expected from a young unmarried woman. It was vaguely flirtatious, and she met the gaze of both men boldly. I was intrigued by her confidence, and a little put out by it too, if I'm honest.

She took a seat between Pepper and Martin, who both appeared to be pleased to find themselves next to her, and I began to wonder exactly what kind of research the men had been doing while I had been playing schoolmistress.

'Thank you for agreeing to see us,' I said.

'Yes ... thank you,' stuttered Martin.

I had never before seen him affected at all by any woman he had come into contact with, and Josephine's considerable influence was something to see in my friend and colleague. Pepper had, fortunately, gathered his wits, and he plunged quickly from the formalities into asking Josephine the questions that we hoped would help us.

'Can you tell us why you left Haven Lee?' Pepper asked.

'You're straight to the point, Mr Pepper,' said Josephine. 'I expected you to warm me up first with a few more pleasantries.'

'Absolutely,' said Martin. 'I'm so sorry if Pepper seems a little rude to you.'

'Not at all,' Josephine said. 'I don't enjoy wasting time. I prefer to be more direct myself. I left the school because … I was afraid.'

'Afraid of what?' I asked. But I thought that I already knew the answer.

'I don't know. I felt anxious all the time. It is difficult to explain. I was sure I was in danger. And every day, that feeling grew worse.'

'How long were you there?' I asked.

'I was there since the age of 14. All was fine in the early years, and then, when I returned after the summer break last year, everything was different.'

'Different how?' asked Pepper.

Josephine shook her head as though to express her own confusion, or perhaps to give herself a moment to reflect.

'I came back a senior. My final year. I was the oldest there. A lot of girls had left by the time they were 16. Parents having other plans for them, I suppose. But mine weren't ready to find me a husband. It's not the French way. We believe in love. Do you believe in love, Mr Crewe?'

'Why … yes,' stuttered Martin.

'And so, they wanted me to have, some final polish I suppose. That last year was to be dedicated to music, needlepoint, and of course to social sophistication. I and two of the other girls, slightly younger than me, would be permitted to go to social gatherings in order to prepare for a coming-out party at the end of the term.

The three of us were looking forward to it. It would also bring us into contact with suitable beaus.'

'Of course,' Martin said.

'But when I returned, the school was *different*. The teachers appeared to be different too, even though they were exactly the same. Mr Dupres was new, of course. And he didn't care for me much, because I picked him up on his French a few times. You know he speaks Creole more than Parisian French, don't you?'

'Yes, I had observed that!' I said. 'Though no-one else seems to be concerned about it.'

'Exactly! It's like they don't notice that something is – off.'

'But *you* noticed?' I prompted.

'Something was *very* wrong. At first I could cope with the small amount of anxiety. I thought I was just nervous. My final year. The whole growing up thing. It was a big deal to me, and the other girls. Mrs Finistra was working with us on dance, Mr Kendal on pianoforte, but Kendal, well ...'

Martin took Josephine's hand as her confident air slipped and she shuddered.

'He was creepy. Kendal, I mean. The music he taught us to play was ... peculiar. It reminded me of ...'

I tried to fill in the blanks for her, because I knew what she meant. I had heard the music. And it wasn't a good or wholesome sound. There was something in it that made me think of ...

'... death,' Josephine continued. 'Funeral music, but worse. I don't know, it is hard to explain. It had a reverent quality, but wasn't like any church music I've ever heard before.'

'I know exactly what you mean,' I said. 'Totally inappropriate.'

'Then the lessons changed. We all had to start attending choir practice more frequently. Not just once a day but every afternoon. Hours and hours of singing. It was exhausting.'

'Do you remember the words of the songs you were singing?' Pepper asked.

'That's the thing, I don't remember any of them. But whenever I heard the music play, I knew *exactly* what to sing. Afterwards it was a blur. Like I had dreamt the whole thing.'

We discussed the music a little more, then Pepper asked Josephine what had happened to spur her finally to leave the school.

'The tension continued to build. It was that feeling you get when it's a really hot summer and there seems to be a storm brewing. It's so humid, it has an impact on your mood. Makes your temper quicker to rise. Makes you feel like you want to shout and stamp your foot. You know?'

We all nodded.

'It was a day like that. Then the evening was worse. As I lay in bed, the air was stifling. I opened the window but the heat that rushed in was somehow worse. It was as if there was no air to breathe, and when you did breathe in, your lungs felt scorched. I tried to sleep, but I just couldn't.

'Eventually I did drift off. Then, all these kind of weird thoughts came into my head. As I was dreaming, I imagined that the school was burning. It grew hotter in the room. The kind of heat that whooshes from the oven when you open the door. I grew certain that fire was licking up the walls around me.

'I jumped awake. When I opened my eyes, the walls of my room were blackened, and smoke floated in the air. I coughed it from my lungs, then staggered to the door to raise the alarm. The building was on fire!

'As I opened the door, however, I saw Mrs Lavender. She was standing at the top of the stairs, just staring at the walls. I glanced back into my room and saw that there was no smoke, no flames. Even though my lungs still burned as though I had inhaled scorching fog.

'I must have been dreaming! "Mrs Lavender," I said. "I had an awful dream!"

'She turned and looked at me then, as though she had only just noticed me. "Did you see that?" she asked me. "Did you see that thing in the wall?"

'I followed her gaze and stared at the wall beside my bedroom door, and I swear it moved. It bulged. Like something was inside, trying to get out. I heard an awful sound, too. Like the slithering of a thousand snakes.

'I think I screamed. And then Mrs Lavender grabbed my hand. She pulled me downstairs. Taking a cloak from her coat-stand by the door, she wrapped it around my shoulders. "You have to leave. Right away. It's marked you. You aren't safe here anymore, Josephine. I can't allow it to take another girl."

'Her words terrified me. I had heard rumours about pupils going missing. And a teacher. But the other girls liked to make up stories like that to scare each other at night, so I had never before taken it seriously. Now I believed it. Something was in there, and it wanted to take me.

'Mrs Lavender opened the door and ran out into the street, leaving me shivering in the vestibule. Then, a few moments later, she returned with a Hansom. She put me inside, pressed money into the hands of the driver and gave him strict instructions to take me to my parents' house, outside of Kingsport, and he wasn't to go anywhere else but there. I think she put the fear of God into him, because he nodded and said he would do what she said.

'By then my fear and anxiety had risen to an extreme level. I was afraid to go home. As we drew farther away from the school, I began to panic. I opened the panel at the front of the cab and demanded that the driver turn back. Thankfully, he ignored my pleas and carried on, driving through the town at breakneck speed. I collapsed back into the seat, exhausted. The fear began to recede as we crossed the border, leaving the town, and it was soon replaced by a terrifying realisation. Mrs Lavender was right. I had been in danger at Haven Lee. I had sensed it, but not understood it. There was an evil presence in that house, and it was affecting all of the students and staff. Even that overwhelming fear of leaving the place was something to do with its terrible influence.'

As she fell silent I became aware of the fact that Martin still held her hand and she had not pulled it away. Now she sat back in her chair, drawing her hand slowly from him, as though she no longer needed the support of this stranger while she told her tale.

'My parents didn't know what to make of my story, of course. Even though I told them everything. They thought I had contracted some kind of brain fever – and I was certainly sick for several weeks after leaving the school.'

'Sick, how?' asked Martin.

'Weakened. Afraid. So exhausted that I could barely leave my bed. It was as though I had consumed a large dose of some sleeping aid. My mind was confused, and I think I said some very peculiar things to my parents, which is why they thought me ill. When I finally came out of it, I refused to go back to the school. I remembered everything and knew I could never return. My parents contacted Mrs Lavender, and she sent them my school fees back with barely more than a few words in a letter, from what they told me.'

After our meeting, Martin walked Josephine back to the hotel reception and made sure she was safely in a cab back home.

'What do you make of all this?' I asked Pepper while Martin was gone.

'Strange. But I guess that's what we knew it would be. That sense of oppression pervading the house, though, I can't imagine what could cause that.'

'Perhaps the school is haunted,' I suggested. 'A ghostly presence could explain the atmosphere. And the illusion that something is in the wall.'

'Perhaps. But I've never heard of a ghost that could influence people to the degree that the teachers and students are affected. Even you have been badly compromised by its power. Usually in ghostly sightings it is only a certain proportion of people that are receptive. The rest see and hear nothing.'

'We don't know that everyone is under its sway. For example, Mrs Finistra seems fairly normal. Perhaps because she gets her weekends back at home and has time to shake the influence. Kendal is involved, though whether willingly or not I'm uncertain. Maybe even Dupres is too. Mrs Lavender has been proven to know more than she's ever been willing to admit, but I doubt that she is behind any of this. After all, why save Josephine? As for the others, they do all appear to be subdued by something. Particularly the students.'

Martin returned to the dining room and rejoined us.

He had similar thoughts about the situation.

'It could be a severe haunting,' Martin said.

'I suppose it is as good a theory as any,' I said. 'But I haven't heard of ghosts kidnapping people before.'

'That's the thing that adds up the least here,' said Martin. 'Ghosts are usually just pranksters. They like to get people in a dither, steal jewellery, appear in the corner of your vision, hide something you are looking for. That kind of thing.'

'You're right,' I said. 'And some instinct tells me this is something else entirely.'

'Something very sinister,' Pepper said.

15

I stayed away from the school for the entire weekend. By Sunday evening I was beginning to feel more like myself again. My analytical skills had returned and I was confident that they wouldn't slip too quickly when I returned to Haven Lee.

I returned after dinner, wanting to avoid the food just in case there was something in it that was dulling my faculties.

'Small doses of laudanum could have an effect on the students. If it was in their food or drink,' Martin had said. 'It is also highly addictive. It might explain why Josephine was so sick and confused on her return home. She would have been suffering from withdrawal symptoms from the drug.'

'You really think they are tampering with the food?' I said.

'Anything is possible. If we rule out the supernatural, then the cause is manmade,' Pepper said.

'And disappearances could be caused by a person rather than a demon of some sort,' I agreed. 'What about Kendal? There is certainly some odd behaviour regarding the choir.'

'I'll investigate further,' Martin said. 'Look into the man's past. But in the meantime, you need to keep the statcom with you at all times.'

'And avoid the cellar,' Pepper reminded.

'I will, when I'm alone. But why don't you two come with me and check it out?'

'What do you have in mind?' Martin had asked.

As I entered the school building I experienced that slight shift in the atmosphere, and a tremor in my heart as anxiety tried to take hold. With renewed vigour, I pushed it down. Now that I recognised it as some other manipulative power, something that was not coming from myself and therefore not a genuine fear, it was much easier to ignore it.

At this hour I realised that the teachers would be gathered in the drawing room, taking their usual dram of port. I didn't join them; instead I went upstairs. I didn't even let anyone know that I was back.

Once in my room with the door locked, I lowered the rope down from my window. Soon afterwards, Pepper and Martin shimmied up and I helped them inside. That night, I planned to take another little walk through the tunnels. But this time I would be armed and I would also have Pepper and Martin with me.

As I pulled the rope back up, there was a knock on my door. Pepper and Martin climbed inside the wardrobe and I pushed the rope under the bed where my visitor wouldn't see it.

I opened the door to find Mrs Lavender there.

'I thought I heard your return. I'm glad you came back,' she said. 'I thought you might want a jug of juice. It's a warm night and it's one of Mrs Harris's rather delicious inventions. It contains elderflower, but she won't reveal any of the other ingredients. I find it helps me sleep.'

'That's very kind of you,' I said, taking the offered jug and placing it on the nightstand. 'And of course I came back. I have a job to do.'

'Perhaps we can talk sometime tomorrow?' she said.

'Yes. I think we really must.'

I closed and locked the door as she left. I had a lot of questions for Mrs Lavender, but now wasn't the time.

Pepper had found the panel behind the wardrobe, and it was already open when I slipped off my skirt, which was, as usual, over a pair of breeches, and climbed into the wardrobe to join them. I took with me several of my favourite weapons.

I was wearing my Remington-Crewe with the laser backpack and I was prepared to use it. The Remington-Crewe had originally been designed by Martin some years earlier. Then he had used diamond shards inside the bullets in order to do maximum damage to a horde of zombies[3]. Now the gun had laser power and could cut a hole through the wall if we needed it to. It also carried a cartridge of bullets, with diamond shards, as we had discovered that diamonds were a powerful deterrent where the supernatural was concerned. And when a ghost-like demon had possessed my brother's wife, Maggie, we had been able to sever its umbilical connection to her using a diamond-shard-coated silver blade[4]. I still had that blade, and it was now safely

---

[3] See *Zombies At Tiffany's*.
[4] See *Kat on a Hot Tin Airship*.

tucked into my ankle sheath, hidden inside my boot.

Even though I didn't need it, I turned on my light bracelet, now fully charged, and followed the men through the back of the wardrobe. As usual Martin had an array of gadgets to light our way in the dark.

Martin studied the passageway carefully as we descended down to the lower ground. He noted all of the secret panels, and confirmed that there was one per room as I had suspected. At the doorway that had previously led me into the pantry, Martin paused. He examined the mechanism to open the panel, then checked the walls all around it. It was then that he discovered another panel, and a staircase that led down to the cellar. We had been planning to enter via the kitchen, but this revelation made it far easier and helped avoid the risk of coming into contact with Harris or Sheppard.

'Of course we may bump into our perpetrator down there,' Pepper pointed out.

'If we do, I'm ready,' I said. I was very willing to exact revenge on the person who had previously pushed me down into the cellar and locked me in, leaving me to some dubious fate. I was also still very cross with myself for having fallen for such an obvious trap. It wasn't like me to have my guard down like that.

The staircase downwards reminded me of the same one I had used to exit the cellar with my rescuer Edward Brewster, and I thought of him now, wishing that I had had enough presence of mind to question him further at the time. Though the meeting now seemed surreal, I knew that I had been in Dalentarth, and I wanted to return there and learn more about Brewster and the place he came from. The world of the Seelie and the Unseelie fascinated me. It would be interesting to learn which court Brewster belonged to, and if the mythology Martin had found bore any resemblance to the real world of the Fae.

We descended the stairs with Martin in the lead, me in the centre and Pepper taking up the rear. Less than ten steps down we came upon a brick wall.

Martin tapped it, searching for a panel to open.

'Looks like this one is closed up,' I said. The closed route to the cellar supported my theory that the house had once been owned by a wealthy family. I mentioned it to the men.

'This must have been a servants' stairway at some time or other. It's too well travelled to have been merely the whim of a wealthy landowner. I must ask Lavender about this place,' I said. 'She may know its history.'

'If it's relevant,' Martin said. 'But I'm not sure it matters.'

'Perhaps not beyond my own curiosity. However, it might be a way to get her talking freely. If she tells me about the history of the house, she may let something else slip while her guard is down.'

'True,' said Pepper.

'Ah. I've found it,' said Martin.

As Martin pressed a loose brick in the wall, another opening appeared.

We found ourselves in a spacious room. In the centre was a large stone altar, but the room was otherwise empty.

'I wasn't expecting this,' I said as we stepped into the room.

The surface of the altar was covered in white symbols. Disc-shaped ones that reminded me of stars.

'It's the Earth,' Martin said. 'Carved into the rock, then painted white. Over and over again in its orbit within our solar system.'

Knowing very little of astronomy I glanced down at the symbols.

'How do you recognise it?' I asked.

Martin raised an eyebrow at me as if to reprimand me for forgetting he is a genius in most things.

'This other one is Saturn. See the rings around it and the extra moons ...'

'Okay, so whoever put this here knows something of astronomy,' Pepper said. 'But that doesn't tell us much.'

'But it does. *This*,' Martin pointed to another set of symbols that looked very different, 'isn't our solar system. I don't know where this is, but our astronomer appears to have discovered other planets not currently known to anyone else in the field.'

'You can't be sure of that,' Pepper said.

'Not sure, no. It could just be ... art of some kind, I suppose,' Martin said. 'The person who carved these likes planets, so he invented some more.'

Martin shrugged as though this idea was more ludicrous than the thought that someone could possibly have discovered an entirely new solar system.

'Ridiculous, then?' I suggested.

'I'm not sure, really. I need to think on it,' Martin said. 'It just doesn't make sense. If there was a way to see further into the sky, don't you think I'd have heard about it by now?'

I had to agree with that. Martin was incredibly well-read. I knew he researched in all areas. As an inventor, he kept abreast with new discoveries. It was unlikely that he wouldn't have heard of such an intriguing discovery.

Leaving Martin to his thoughts, I turned my attention back to the room, which was, as I had first assumed, completely empty bar a curtain that covered another door. This door was made of solid oak and had a thick mortise lock, which was part of a large iron handle.

'It's locked,' Martin said. Then he removed a small pouch that was hanging from his tool belt. Inside were his lock picks.

It took him only a few seconds to fool the mechanism into believing that it was turning for the proper key, before he pulled open the door and we entered the main cellar. I glanced back at the brick opening we had passed through, and noted that it had closed behind us. I hoped that it would be possible to go back out through there if need be.

It was dark and dreary in the cellar. We passed furniture covered with off-white dust sheets. I recognised a bureau, a few chairs, a coat-stand and a table among the shadows. It was just as you might expect a basement to look, in a house as substantial as this, and we moved through this room trying to get our bearings.

'I assume you don't recognise any of this stuff?' Pepper asked.

'No. We have to be on the side that I didn't see.'

In the next room I found the coal hatch. It was irritating to realise that I had merely turned the wrong way before, and could so easily have got out of the cellar if I had gone left instead of right.

'The hatch is unlocked,' Pepper observed. 'And it looks as though they have just had a new delivery of coal and logs.'

The room smelt of coal: dark, dusky. I liked the smell. Like the cellar itself, the coal had a kind of cold, damp odour that wasn't unpleasant.

We passed through a few more rooms and glanced

into the wine cellar, which was as well stocked as I recalled. Then we found ourselves by the stairs that led legitimately up to the kitchen. The same stairs I had been so ruthlessly thrown down.

Now with Pepper and Martin with me, the cellar did not seem so daunting. It was familiar instead, and fear comes only from things that we don't know or understand.

'I want to see that room you were herded into,' Martin said. 'And the panel that Edward Brewster opened up to rescue you.

I led the way. Once at the door, though, I was reluctant to go inside.

'I'll stay here and guard the door,' I suggested. 'The last thing we need is for it to be closed again. We can't guarantee that Edward Brewster will be around this time to open it from the other side.'

Pepper and Martin went inside, but first Pepper wedged a chair against the heavy door to keep it open. I sat down on the chair and looked back at the route we had taken, pointing my Remington-Crewe laser in that direction, so that I would be ready if my attacker appeared.

Martin walked the perimeter of the room, examining all of the walls. Now that we knew what the panels looked like, and mostly how they operated, I expected him to find something quickly.

The room was disappointingly bare, however. The only exit point he found was the same one that had been opened for me by Edward Brewster, and Martin, like me, could find no way of getting through it.

'I guess Brewster was telling the truth when he said that only he could open the door,' I said.

'Sadly,' said Pepper. 'Except that we could probably

use the laser to get through.'

'True, but that would then open this route permanently, and I'm sure that the occupants of Dalentarth wouldn't be too happy about that,' I pointed out.

'Well. This has been something of a wasted trip,' Martin said.

'Welcome to my world,' I commented. 'It feels as though most of the searches I've done recently have led nowhere.'

'We do now have the lie of the land down here,' Pepper said. 'That's a bonus. I would like to go back to the first room. Get another look at that stone altar. There's something about it that is niggling me.'

'Good plan,' Martin said.

I placed the chair back were Martin had found it, and we returned quickly through the cellar and back to the first room. But as we approached the door, which was once more closed, I could hear that strange off-kilter music that Kendal had been playing for his choir.

There was candlelight filtering under the door and flickering shadows as the music abruptly halted.

Following a gut instinct, we all hid among the cloth-covered furniture. I had just ducked down behind the table when the door opened.

From my vantage point I could see into the room beyond. It was now lit with candles all around the edges. There was a harpsichord in the corner near the panel that led to the staircase in the hidden passage. I found it difficult to fathom how the room could have been dressed with so many candles and several pieces of furniture in such a short space of time. On the altar there was now a chalice, a sharp looking knife and a round, shallow bowl.

It appeared to be the makings of a ceremony.

My view was obscured then by a figure in a long, red, monk-like robe. It appeared to be a man, judging by height and build, but I could not see who it was, because he had a thick cowl pulled up over his head. The light from the candles behind him revealed only his shape and height, which appeared to be elongated by shadow. Where the face should have been I could see only a black void.

A line of similarly robed people passed through the room in front of the table. The three of us crouched lower, and I hoped that we wouldn't be seen. The robed figures passed by us with heads bowed and hands hidden inside their sleeves like pious monks. They went through the door and drew into a circle around the altar. Then the door closed and our room was plunged into darkness as the bizarre music started up in the altar room once more.

16

The coal hatch was now open and moonlight shone down onto the coal cellar steps. Martin edged closer to the door as I looked out into the other room from which the strange worshippers had emerged. It was obvious that they had entered not from the school building but down the steps from outside, which meant that they might be completely unconnected with the school and just using this room for their bizarre rituals.

Chanting and music came from the altar room, and peculiar images flashed behind my eyes. I saw a dark, desolate landscape, with black fungus growing over rocky terrain. In the distance I perceived a tall rock formation, and I likened it to the crystal fortress I had seen on the horizon at Dalentarth. Only this was a place of night, not of light and beauty.

'Kat? Are you all right?' Martin said.

Martin was beside me, and Pepper quickly joined him, taking my arm.

'What's wrong?'

'Nothing. A vision, I think. Something that the music and chanting are making me see.'

Martin and Pepper exchanged a look.

'What do you see?' Pepper asked.

'A black rock formation. A foreign landscape. Like nothing I have ever seen. A place that you would expect to find in haunting fairytales.'

'A dream world?' Martin asked.

'No. This place is real,' I said. '*Look.*'

I pointed upwards towards the coal hatch opening. Martin and Pepper turned. The skyline had changed. I hurried up the steps, and Pepper and Martin followed, as though we were all drawn against our will. I had to see why the sky appeared to be so different. What had changed?

At the top I found the landscape of my vision. Dark night, with a moonless sky. A shaft of light, though, extended from the top of the rock formation. It was like a beacon, or a lighthouse light. Only this light held something sinister within it that I just couldn't fathom.

The sky was bereft of stars, yet cloudless. I was a moth, drawn to a flame, even though I knew it would burn me. I found myself stepping out onto the fungal landscape. The texture of the ground was sticky, and it sucked at my boots as I walked on it.

'Wait!' Martin said. 'We shouldn't …'

Silence. Not even the howling of wind. It was as though the atmosphere absorbed sound.

'What do you make of …?' I began to say, but my voice was stolen as soon as it passed my lips.

I looked back behind me and discovered that my friends, and the coal hatch, had completely disappeared.

I was alone, and I knew this was not some countryside near the school or, I realised with unprecedented surety, even on my own planet. A flash of memory, a vision of the planetary systems carved on the altar, surfaced behind my eyes. I was there!

Wherever that was. Somehow I had crossed into another world.

An awful anxiety bloomed in my breast. Panic surged inside me. I was on my own. And I had no way of getting back.

The ground squelched beneath me as I backed up to where the hatch had been. It was damp, cloying. Tendrils wrapped around my ankles and began to tug at me, almost pulling me off my feet.

I looked down to see that the ground was moving. The vile, black fungus was shaping into something that resembled plant life, and it was crawling up my legs, trying to gain purchase for some weird purpose I couldn't understand.

I realised that this *was* foliage of a sort, like tree roots thrusting up from the ground. Only these roots grew quickly and had a motivation. That purpose right now was somehow to wrap themselves around me.

I pulled the Remington-Crewe laser from its holster and directed it down towards the ground. Then I fired two short bursts. The laser light sparked briefly, but all sound was absent as the gun expelled its powerful beam. The plant-tendrils shrivelled and burnt, sinking back into the ground, only to be followed by a burst of new ones that crawled around and gripped my boots until I was forced to fire the laser again.

This place was dangerous. I had to find some shelter and then, hopefully, a way back.

At that moment a hand grabbed at my arm. I was yanked backwards before I had an opportunity to react, and I found myself tumbling down the steps, back into the cellar.

My landing was soft, however, as Pepper caught me. Falling to the ground beneath my body, he buffered the impact.

Martin helped me to my feet. I was bruised and shocked, and the Remington-Crewe had been knocked from my grasp. It tumbled down the stairs behind me with a brief clatter, then landed at my feet.

'We almost lost you there,' Pepper said, pulling himself up from the ground. 'Please don't cross any of these doorways again until we know exactly what they are and where they lead.'

I brushed the coal dust from my breeches, reflecting that it was fortunate I was wearing black. I was disorientated, and it took a few moments for the sound of chanting to reach my ears once more.

'What happened on the other side?' asked Pepper.

'The hatch disappeared,' I said.

'I thought so. We could still see you. But you clearly couldn't see us, which is why I reached through for you,' Pepper explained.

'What *was* that?' I asked.

'At a guess, I'd say a gateway into another dimension,' Martin said.

'Another world …' I said.

'If you like,' Martin agreed. 'Perhaps it even was another planet. Look … It's gone now.'

I looked back up towards the hatch and saw the moon shining from a clear, star-filled sky. It was a relief to see my own world above us.

'I think you're right,' I said. 'That was a door to another planet. It was awful. Barren. Dark. Rotten. I could feel evil seeping from the ground beneath my feet. The plant-life tried to take hold of me.'

The chanting stopped in the room beyond.

'Let's get out of here,' Pepper suggested. 'Or at least take cover again.'

The door to the altar room opened and the three of us hurried ahead, passing back through the various cellar rooms before taking shelter behind the racks of bottles in the wine cellar.

The entourage passed by without looking into the room, buy then one of them halted. The robed shape came into the wine cellar and paused by the rack of port. Then he or she lifted up a bottle. From within the sleeve of the robe, the figure pulled out a thick syringe. Forcing the needle in through the cork, he or she discharged the syringe's contents into the bottle. As the needle was removed again, a strong, bitter odour filled the room. The robed figure hid the syringe once more, then left the wine cellar, taking the port bottle too.

Then he or she joined the others as they left the cellar via the stairs that led directly to the kitchen. In my mind, this confirmed that they had to be some, or all, of the teachers. Somehow they were all involved in this.

Pepper, Martin and I waited until there was no more sound and then, by unspoken agreement, made our way back to the altar room.

'What do you think they put into the port?' Pepper asked.

'Laudanum. Without a doubt,' said Martin. 'And I suspect doses of it are also in the food.'

'But why?' I said.

'It will make everyone more pliable; and the less psychic among the residents, a little more receptive.'

'It also explains Josephine Boulogne's sickness. As we suspected, it was withdrawal symptoms,' Pepper said.

'Yes,' said Martin.

As we passed through the coal cellar we noticed that the hatch was now closed again. And the altar room door was once more locked. Martin pressed his ear against the door and listened for a while until he was satisfied that no-one was inside. Then he picked the lock as before.

The room was bare again, with nothing to evidence that the robed worshippers had been there. It was inconceivable that the harpsichord and candles could all have disappeared. Where had they gone?

'Not possible,' said Martin, voicing my thoughts. 'Perhaps they took it all through the secret passage.'

Pepper hurried across the room and, without effort, slid the panel open. We all peered through the entrance that had first brought us into this room. There was no sign of anyone else having used this way.

I stepped back, and the heel of my boot found something that our eyes had not detected: spilt wax. It was on the ground beside the altar. I knelt down and daubed my fingers in the red liquid, only to discover it wasn't wax at all. It was blood.

'Martin,' I said, holding up my finger to show him.

Both he and Pepper hurried to my side as I stood up again. We examined the altar. Now that we were focused on it, we could see that fresh blood had seeped into the carved symbols, turning the white red. But even as we watched, the red faded, as though absorbed into the stone.

'Kat!' Martin said.

'What?' I looked at him, bemused.

'Your … fangs have grown,' Pepper said.

I didn't like to see that expression on Pepper's face. He looked afraid, but not just of the situation we were in. He was frightened of me.

17

I was subdued as we returned through the tunnels and back to my room. The fangs had slipped back into my gums once I had realised they were there, but Martin and Pepper had become uncharacteristically quiet. I knew what they were thinking though: it was the sight and feel of the blood that I had reacted to. Though I knew this wasn't true. I had felt no hunger at the sight of the blood, though I had been distressed to find it on the altar. I had also felt my instinct to destroy evil rise up.

'Someone must have been sacrificed,' Martin said as we reached the passageway for my floor and halted outside the door that led into my wardrobe.

'The thought of it is horrifying,' I said. 'Could it have been the missing Hilary?'

'Lavender told you she was coming back this week, didn't she?' Pepper asked.

'Yes. She did.'

'Then we can only wait and see if she does return,' Martin said.

'Do you think that we have discovered some kind of Satanic cult?' I asked.

'More than likely,' Pepper said. 'This is terrible. How

am I going to tell Colonel Baker that Shirley-Anne has probably been used as some kind of human sacrifice, to some unknown evil?'

I hung my head. This was not the conclusion we had hoped for. We had wanted to find the girl, uncover what was happening at Haven Lee and prevent it from occurring again.

'I can't believe that we were outside that room all the time that someone was being murdered,' Pepper said.

'It's too horrible,' I said. I felt like a failure, and I was sure that Pepper and Martin had an equal amount of guilt.

'It's not over yet,' Martin said. 'We don't know that she is dead, or that anyone else is.'

'It's not that far a leap though,' I said. 'Considering all the things we've seen that the Darkness has sprung into this world.'

'Is the Darkness behind this, then?' Pepper asked. 'Only this *feels* different to me. It feels … other.'

'Not of this world, you mean?' I said.

Pepper nodded. 'Something from the other world we saw tonight, perhaps.'

'But how do you know that the place wasn't hell? Or some other demon realm?' I asked.

'Well, I think it *was* a demon realm,' Martin said. 'That's the thing. And all the discussions we've had in the past about hell dimensions have, in a way, been proved more than just theories tonight.'

'True,' I said.

After we had passed through the wardrobe back into my room, I encouraged Pepper and Martin to leave so that I could get some sleep. I was exhausted.

'I'm not very comfortable with the idea of leaving you here alone,' Pepper said.

'We've been through all that already. And unless I stay, we are never going to get to the bottom of this. We will fail Shirley-Anne and all of the other women and girls that have vanished.'

Reluctantly my companions left, climbing down the rope from my bedroom window.

I pulled the thick cord back up, untied it from around the sturdy bed and stowed it in the bottom of my trunk.

Taking my nightdress out of the top drawer in the bureau, I noticed the jug of juice that Mrs Lavender had brought to me earlier. I had no intention of drinking from it, or eating or drinking anything provided by the school from now on. The last thing I needed was my senses being dulled by laudanum. I sniffed the jug and detected a bitter odour. But never having come across any form of opiate before, I couldn't be certain that there was anything dangerous lurking within the contents.

Unable to think on it any further, I undressed and climbed into the bed, falling asleep almost immediately.

A tentative knock pulled me from the nightmarish reliving of my brief experience in the dark world. In my dream that awful weed, gripping my ankles, had managed to pull me to the ground. I was being dragged down into the vile-smelling earth, choking on the thick black fungus as it poured into my mouth when I tried to scream for help. Of course, in this nightmare, Pepper and Martin were nowhere near. My confused and sleeping brain had seen them left behind in the cellar with no way to reach me.

It was still dark outside, but it was a relief to be woken. Even as I climbed from my bed, wiping fever perspiration from my brow before it could drip into my eyes, I found it difficult to shake the terror of that awful place from my conscious mind.

I opened the door to find Mrs Lavender on the other side.

'I need to talk to you,' she said.

'And I need to talk to you too,' I answered.

I pulled on my robe and, locking the door behind me, followed Mrs Lavender downstairs to her office. I had at first thought it odd that she wanted me to go down there, when we could have spoken in my room just as easily, but as she had darted nervous glances towards the wardrobe, it had reaffirmed to me that she knew about the secret passageway.

Once in her office I remained standing. I didn't feel the need to put myself in the chair opposite her desk, though I was unsure why.

'Miss Lightfoot,' she began.

'Please call me Kat,' I said.

'It has come to my attention that something is seriously wrong at Haven Lee. I'll get straight to the point and say that I think Mr Kendal is involved. He has been behaving strangely and … have you heard the peculiar songs that he is teaching our students?'

My mind was racing. Lavender was relating to me all of my own observations, but her voice held no emotion, unlike during our last conversation when I had felt that perhaps I had misjudged her. I also knew, from Josephine Boulogne's account that Mrs Lavender had known all along that something strange was happening at Haven Lee. She had rescued Josephine, after all, and this had made her appear to me as trustworthy. However, that awkward nervousness was seeping into my psyche again and I was experiencing a vague emotion that I recognised as paranoia.

I saw Mrs Lavender's gaze go to the stationery cupboard behind me and wondered if she was feeling the same. After my thorough exploration of the passageway with Martin and Pepper, my earlier suspicion that an entrance existed behind it had been confirmed.

'Whatever do you mean?' I answered, playing the innocent until I was certain whether she was friend or foe.

'You must have noticed. Things are not right here.'

My eyes fell on a bottle of port that sat on Mrs Lavender's desk. I had a flash of recall of the gloved hand that had taken the bottle from the wine cellar, and contaminated it, a few hours earlier. It seemed obvious to me at that moment that Mrs Lavender must have been that person. Perhaps this whole conversation was her way of establishing whether or not I knew anything?

With this suspicion in mind, I was determined to keep my own counsel. There were several questions I wanted to ask her, especially about Josephine, but they would have to wait until the right moment, when I would either trust her, or catch her off guard.

'How long have you been suspicious of ... Mr Kendal?' I asked.

'Oh ... a while. He came to us with excellent references. Though that was before my time, of course.'

'I'm sure he did. But what is it you think he's doing?'

'I think he may be kidnapping young girls for some nefarious purpose,' Mrs Lavender said.

Then, she blushed. It was an interesting reaction, one that suggested knowledge of what that nefarious purpose was. Or perhaps it was guilt that she had been unable to protect the pupils.

And indeed, it was obvious that Kendal was involved

on some level too, though how far in he was, was something that still needed to be determined. The fact that Mrs Lavender was pointing the finger at him made me wonder even more about her contribution to the whole thing.

'I'm not sure why you're telling me this,' I said. 'I've been here just a week and I barely know any of the teachers. I don't think that Mr Kendal and I have even spoken.'

'I don't know why, but I trust you. I think you can help me.'

'Help you, how?'

'I can't go to the authorities with this. If they don't lock me up as insane, then they might arrest me for not going to them sooner.'

'That's all possible,' I agreed. 'But you could say that you had only recently become aware that there was a problem.'

'I could. But I'd be lying.'

Mrs Lavender's eyes began to water. I could see now that her apparent lack of feeling had resulted from the sheer will of holding her emotions in check.

But what about the port? What had she been doing among those robed worshippers the night before? Should I lay my cards on the table and just ask her outright? Would she confirm that laudanum had been put into the bottle?

I decided against playing my hand. The time wasn't right, and Mrs Lavender would have to tell me more before I could really assess her motives.

'The thing is, Kat, because you are new here, I know you aren't involved. I can't trust anyone else. You're the only one I can talk to about this.'

Her tone was sincere, and *I believed her.* My eyes

skipped over the port bottle once more. Then Mrs Lavender's eyes fell on it.

'What on earth is this doing here?' she said. Then she glanced once more at the wardrobe.

She picked up the dusty bottle. I noticed that the finger marks, obviously left by the person who had last touched it, did not match Mrs Lavender's at all. Her hands were larger. This meant that the perpetrator was more than likely a female, but smaller in build than Mrs Lavender.

I decided that I had to hurry things along, and that meant admitting to my suspicions.

'Okay. Let's cut to the chase,' I said. 'You need to tell me everything you know about this house.'

'Why?'

'Because I agree with you, something isn't right here. And I intend to find out what it is.'

'Who are you?' she asked. Her eyes peered into mine as though she were attempting to read my thoughts – something that I believed wasn't possible. Then, as though defeated, she sat back in her chair.

'The thing is,' I said, 'you know who I am. It's I who should be asking you that question.'

Mrs Lavender stared off into the darkest corner of the room for a moment. Then she began to tell me her story.

'The house was built over a hundred years ago,' Mrs Lavender explained. 'It was the vision of a wealthy landowner by the name of Carter Forsyth. In those days Kingsport was known as Salt Lick. Rumour has it that before Forsyth came to Salt Lick he had made his money in gold mines. Somehow he came to settle here, though it isn't known why, and then he built his first ranch.

'This house – and I'm sure you could tell it wasn't purpose-built as a school – was designed for his young bride.

'She was called Emelia Jane Carmichael and she was twenty years his junior, but from all the stories I've been told, Forsyth loved her and wanted to make her happy. You see, Emelia was used to social life, something living on a ranch outside of town couldn't give her. She was from a good family too, but her family didn't have the accumulated wealth of Forsyth, and that was, I suppose, how he managed to broker the deal of procuring her for his wife. It was the way things were done then. To an extent, of course, they still are.

'Forsyth found the land first. And he got it for a bargain price. No-one wanted to live here, as there were rumours about it being … haunted …'

'Haunted in what way?' I asked.

'There were reports of women going missing from the surrounding plots of land. One or two turned up again, but they were confused and couldn't explain what had happened. There was talk of witchcraft, or maybe it was just Cherokee magic. People were so credulous in those days that this sort of thing just grew from idle gossip into a full-blown superstition.'

'I understand. It is still like that in some parts …' I said.

I urged Mrs Lavender to continue, holding back all of the questions I wanted to ask her.

'So, Forsyth built Haven Lee. And for a time he lived here with Emelia. They had their social gatherings, and Emelia's parents even came to stay permanently in the house, as did Forsyth's own ageing mother.

'It wasn't long before things started to go wrong for them, though. It was the disappearance of a young house maid that started the real trouble. The maid's parents lived in Salt Lick, by the river, and they hadn't been too happy about their daughter going to work at Haven Lee. They were superstitious, fanatically religious people, sprung from the early Quaker settlers. This branch of the family had somehow found its way to Tennessee. Perhaps they had been attracted by the promise of wealth and land.

'Still, they were a poor family, and the girl had been forced to find and take the only work available in the area that wasn't too backbreaking. It must have seemed like a dream job to her at the time. Her only other option would have been working on the land. I know which choice I'd have made.'

Mrs Lavender paused, as though she held a real understanding of the girl's plight. I waited for her to continue, though I must admit I didn't understand where this story was taking us. It didn't matter, though, because I knew it was going somewhere, that it did have a point. In my experience, stories always lead to some important revelation; you just have to have some patience when listening to them.

'So the girl went missing …' I prompted when Mrs Lavender's pause became too long.

'Yes. Her name was Miriam. Miriam Lancaster,' Mrs Lavender continued. 'And she was my great grandmother.'

She paused again, giving me time to absorb this new piece of information.

'Go on,' I said, impatient now, despite my earlier resolve to let her tell her story in her own time!

'Miriam was found eventually. But she wasn't the same girl that had entered Haven Lee. She had become paranoid, afraid. She was hysterical even, and she talked of crazy things. Her parents refused to let her go into an asylum, even though doctors advised it. Instead they kept her home and nursed her back to health. After a couple of years, when the whole sordid business was forgotten, Miriam married and then went on to have a daughter of her own. That was my grandmother, Rachel Bales. Rachel married Joseph Adams, and then she gave birth to Daphne. Daphne Adams married a man called Ebenezer Sykes. These were my parents.

'I suppose you are wondering why this is relevant? Well, I'll tell you. Miriam died in childbirth, but she left a letter for Rachel, and that letter was passed down to my mother and eventually to me. It told of an unspeakable horror that lurked underground. Of a gateway into hell. My great-grandmother was sent there by a group of evil people. Witches, she called them, but in her lifetime she had been afraid to speak of it for fear of being institutionalised. Plus, those so-called witches, a formed coven, had been from very powerful families.

'When Miriam learned she was pregnant, she grew afraid for her unborn child. She had to leave this warning behind to ensure that none of her family returned to the house. She feared that they would be at greater risk than anyone else.'

'If that's so, then why are *you* here?' I asked.

'My mother didn't give me the letter from my great-grandmother until it was too late. By then I had sent Lucy, my daughter, to Haven Lee. Its reputation was exceptional, and I had thought it the best thing for her. When Lucy disappeared, my mother gave me the letter. She was ashamed that she hadn't revealed the family secret to me sooner, though I suspect that even if she had done, I would have taken it with a pinch of salt.

'Unlike some of the missing girls, Lucy never came back.'

'I'm so sorry,' I said. 'I can't imagine how this must feel for you.'

'Six months ago, I came here with the intention of learning the truth; but as you can imagine, it has been almost impossible to do. I suspect everyone. And even new employees over the years appear to have changed and become involved in this … conspiracy.'

'That's why you have been so distrustful of me,' I said.

'Exactly. But I'm taking a risk now, because, Miss Lightfoot … Kat …, I believe you are different.'

'I'd like to see this family letter if I could,' I said.

'Of course! I have it in my room. If you wait here, I will go and fetch it.'

She hurried from the office then, and I surveyed the room casually in her absence while I thought about her story. It all sounded plausible, though I had to consider that it could still be some kind of deception designed to make me reveal what I knew. But I wasn't planning to do that anytime soon, no matter how sincere Mrs Lavender's story seemed to be. Not until I was confident that she wasn't involved. After all, she could have been one of the robed worshippers, and this could all be a ruse.

When many minutes passed by, I began to wonder how long it was going to take Mrs Lavender to return. I could see light peeking through the curtains in the office window. Dawn was approaching, and in less than an hour there would be activity in the school that would endanger the privacy of our meeting.

I went to the office door, looked out into the hallway. Then the hairs stood up on the back of my neck. I had a peculiar concern for Mrs Lavender. If her story was true, then surely she was as much in danger here as her daughter Lucy had been. But how had she remained safe so far, if that was the case?

I found myself hurrying up the stairs and along the landing to Mrs Lavender's room before I even consciously decided to go in search of her. I was just aware that her errand was taking her far too long.

My canines sprang from my gums with a sharp burst of discomfort. I touched them with my fingertips, then explored them with my tongue. It was an interesting realisation that, if there was to be some sort of battle, I did have my own inbuilt daggers, and I knew with a certainty that they would cause some damage: this was my new defence mechanism.

Even so, as I arrived at Mrs Lavender's door, I retrieved the silver and diamond-shard dagger from my boot and entered the room with the weapon in my hand. You could never have enough knives as far as I was concerned.

It took me barely a few seconds to realise that Mrs Lavender had been taken. The wardrobe in her room was open. And I could hear the awful rattle and slither of what sounded like a nest of vipers.

Without thought of what I would find, I plunged into the wardrobe in pursuit of Mrs Lavender's kidnapper.

18

The passageway showed signs of struggle. This was evident in the smears in the dust, and there was a vile green slime tarnishing the inside of the wardrobe. It looked to me as though Mrs Lavender had been pulled roughly through the wardrobe, and was now being dragged down into the cellar.

I could hear that unpleasant sound again. It wasn't a sound that humans made, and it brought that irrational fear up into my chest, even though the adrenaline rush pushed it back down again. My fangs ached in my gums. But I still wasn't feeling the vampire bloodlust in the sense that those awful creatures who had infected me had. This was me spoiling for a fight. A fight with a foe that I didn't understand, and the thought both scared and thrilled me.

I heard a muffled cry and followed the sound. Mrs Lavender was in danger and I wouldn't allow another woman to be taken if I could help it.

I reached the flight of stairs leading to the ground floor and hurried down them. Then I ran full pelt down the corridor towards the staircase that led to the altar room in the cellar.

Mrs Lavender's captor always stayed ahead of me, and as I arrived at this final staircase I heard the panel to the altar room closing below.

I took the stairs two at a time and reached the bottom in seconds, then I searched for the opening and was soon pushing my way through the door into the altar room.

I stopped as I saw the altar shifting back into place, and then I realised our error from the night before. There was another passageway, and it was beneath this slab of stone.

How it opened I could only guess. I kicked, pushed, searched. But could find nothing to suggest a way to move it.

At that moment my statcom buzzed. I fished it out of my clothing and answered.

'Just thought I'd check in with you,' said Pepper. 'I had the strangest feeling.'

'You need to get here. Lavender has been taken,' I said. 'And I've found another passageway.'

It didn't take long for Pepper and Martin to reach me. I met them at the front door, and we all hurried downstairs to the altar room via the stationary cupboard entrance in Mrs Lavender's office. As we passed by the entrance to the kitchen pantry, I could hear the clatter and bustle just starting up in there as Mrs Harris began to make breakfast. The students and teachers were oblivious to Mrs Lavender's disappearance, and I intended for it to remain that way for the time being.

In the altar room, Martin, being our resident genius, studied the altar, while Pepper and I loaded up with weapons.

While I had been waiting for the men to arrive I had

retrieved my carpetbag and changed into my fighting gear. I was wearing a white shirt, a red bodice and my favourite men's breeches and knee-length boots. I strapped on my weapons belt, from which hung my crossbow and a cartridge of diamond-shard bullets: expensive weaponry, but useful when fighting the forces of the Darkness.

'I think it's something to do with the planetary alignment,' Martin said.

'It looks correct to me,' Pepper said.

'Our planetary alignment is. But what about this one?' Martin said.

He probed the carvings of the strange solar system, fingers running in and out of the grooves like a blind man reading Braille.

Then he found a tiny nodule, barely noticeable in the stone, but off-kilter with the rest once it was seen. Martin pressed it. Nothing happened and, exasperated, he stepped back. The heel of his shoe caught in a small, raised fragment of what had appeared to be a broken stone slab on the floor. The fragment sank into the ground, and the top surface of the altar shifted.

As Martin had said, the alignment of the planets was wrong, and now they moved, and swirled, like magic, without the slightest change to the physical altar itself. It was as though an image floated over the altar. Overlapping it, like two objects occupying the same space. The illusion was fascinating: an impossible trick.

A dull light glowed beneath the stone. The altar seemed to shift, but I began to wonder if it really did move at all, or if it was merely a change in my perception. Maybe it had never moved in the first place, and that was why I had been unable to find a way to pursue Mrs Lavender's captor.

But, a gateway *was* opening.

Martin, Pepper and I found ourselves looking down into the bowels of the earth as a row of steps appeared to unravel beneath our feet, right where the altar had been. I had an awareness that the altar was still there, but it was the stone that was an image overlaying the steps now.

As our shift in space settled, I was the first to begin to climb down. My fangs had retracted as I had waited for my friends to arrive, and my adrenaline had calmed a little. Now the fangs came through again, slowly, less painfully, and far more controlled than the previous times that they had appeared. I was learning to manage the metamorphosis far better now, and I wanted my new weapons ready to use.

Pepper and Martin were on my heels as I traversed the steps. They were cut from solid rock. The air was thinner here. I could smell that sickly black weed that had clawed at me when I had passed through to this world through the coal hatch. Even so, there was no sign of the fungus. The steps were like those leading to a catacomb. Would we find the remains of the dead down here along with whoever or whatever had taken Mrs Lavender?

'It's a different dimension all right,' Martin confirmed.

'Good. There is sound down here at least,' I said.

'What do you mean?' asked Pepper. 'Of course there is.'

'There wasn't any above ground in this place. It seemed to be a vacuum.'

'Unusual,' said Martin. 'But not surprising. This world is everything ours isn't. It is darkness. Even the light – and there is light, strangely – feels like shadow.'

'I know what you mean,' I said. 'It's as though dark is

light, light is dark, exact opposites.'

'Precisely,' Martin said. 'Yin to our yang, I suppose.'

We seemed to be descending for a long time. I was concerned that whatever fate had been waiting for Mrs Lavender, had already occurred, and that we would be too late.

I hurried down the steps faster. Martin and Pepper kept pace with me, though I knew that this was a problem for Pepper with his old war injury. Even so, he made no complaint as he hurried after us.

The steps changed direction now, and without a shift of pace we were climbing, not descending. The air became heavier and, although it barely affected me, I noticed that my companions struggled with it.

'We are almost there,' I said, trying to encourage them.

I wasn't simply being optimistic when I said it, either: I was sure we were near. When the steps curved once more downwards we came to their end, and found ourselves in a large chamber.

'Where are we?' Pepper said. His voice was a whisper, yet the high-ceilinged chamber picked up the sound and echoed it around above our heads.

I pressed a hand to my lips, warning of making any more noise, lest our presence be noticed. We needed time to explore this place, and hopefully to determine who had taken Mrs Lavender before we were discovered. We needed the element of surprise on our side.

The room was curved, almost perfectly round, with just one doorway leading off on the other side, clearly marked by an ornate arch. It was devoid of furnishing, little more than an empty cavern, but as I took a step forward there was a further shift in time and space, and this abnormal dimension altered around us.

We were now in what resembled a ballroom. A room not dissimilar to the dining room at Haven Lee. For a moment I thought we had passed back into our own realm, and I glanced at Pepper and Martin, who were either side of me, to see their reaction. Both wore a similar expression that conveyed a mutual feeling of confusion and amazement. The phenomenon did not last for long, however, and no sooner had I turned my eyes over this whole new room, than it had changed back into the empty chamber.

'A dimension slip,' Martin murmured, and his voice was caught and carried around in a flurry of loud echoes way beyond anything that should have been possible with so low a whisper.

'It's opposite,' I said, speaking loudly.

My voice didn't echo, and my companions caught onto my observation and began to talk as noisily as possible.

'This is all so improbable,' Martin said. 'But fascinating. This place is like the anti-world.'

'What did you make of that flash of Haven Lee's ballroom?' I asked.

'It was like a reflection, or an old captured image. Not really here at all,' said Martin. 'Perhaps … No, that would be insane.'

'Tell us anyway,' shouted Pepper.

'I think this whole area is an anomaly,' Martin said. 'It is as though it is a bridge, a gateway, or even some kind of corner where the dimensions collide.'

Now that he had spoken it, I suspected that his thoughts were close to the truth. It might also explain why there had been disappearances in the area before the house was built there, and why, when some of those victims had returned, they had been confused and afraid. Walking from one world accidentally into another would make anyone fear they had lost their minds, let alone an innocent who knew nothing of demon worlds and the Darkness.

'I felt, when the altar disappeared and the steps arrived, that they were two places occupying the same space,' I said.

'I've always suspected that many dimensions lie over each other,' Martin said. 'This all seems to confirm that my theories were valid.'

A muffled sob echoed through the chamber.

'Where was that coming from?' I said in a normal tone, forgetting to be loud. My voice bounced around the room.

Martin crossed the chamber, heading towards the door on the opposite side. Pepper and I followed, and as our friend reached the door, the shift in the chamber happened again.

'There must be another gateway,' I said.

Music echoed around the room.

'The choir are singing,' I said. 'In the school.'

'That's awful,' said Pepper, covering his ears.

The music made my head ache, and by the look on Martin's face I could tell he found the experience wholly unpleasant too.

'They don't usually rehearse in the morning. And, how can we even hear them down here?' I said.

'Of course!' Martin said. 'The choir. The music. They are chanting some mystical spell that opens the gateway and thins the barrier so much that it converges the two dimensions.'

'That doesn't sound healthy,' Pepper said.

'Not at all good,' Martin said. 'Very dangerous to our world. And, if they have been chanting so much of late, it explains those little slips into the other realm. Like through the coal hatch. The barrier between worlds is becoming compromised. If this continues much longer we may not be able to stop a complete overlap.'

'What will happen then?' I asked.

'The world will not be ours anymore,' Martin said, confirming my fears.

The music grew louder, my ears began to ring and Martin and Pepper groaned in distress and pain.

'We have to stop this,' I yelled.

I untucked my shirt from my breeches and ripped a strip of the cloth from the bottom. Then, I tore the strip into four pieces and gave two each to the men.

'Here,' I said. 'Block your ears.'

They took the fabric and stuffed it into their ears. I didn't need to do the same. The music was uncomfortable for me to listen to but not creating the same debilitating pain that my friends were suffering.

'That helps a little,' Martin shouted.

'It's horrible,' complained Pepper, and I almost laughed at the absurdity of it. It was horrible and totally ridiculous, and I had never known Pepper to take such a dislike to any form of music before.

Another small cry came through the doorway. As we moved towards it the music grew louder, and I realised it was somehow trying to prevent us from crossing the threshold. This made me realise that there must be something important beyond it. Perhaps this was exactly where Mrs Lavender had been taken.

Grabbing hold of the hands of my colleagues, I pulled them both towards the door.

Blissful silence descended as we passed under the stone archway. We were in another chamber, only this one was smaller.

Ahead of us I saw a row of arches, each of them with bars across it, forming a large cage: a possible prison cell.

From this distance I could see stacks of hay inside the enclosures.

'Animals?' I said, and was relieved when my voice didn't echo.

'Let's take a look,' said Martin as he removed the fabric from his ears.

The first cell was empty, but the hay was piled in one corner as though it were a makeshift bed. In the second we saw a small figure lying on a similar pile.

I pulled my dagger from my ankle holster and jammed it into the lock before Martin had time to search for his lock picks. The lock broke easily and I hurried inside, crouching down beside the figure.

'Mrs Lavender?' I said. I reached a hand towards the shoulder of the figure and she turned and looked at me. It was Deborah Darlington. 'Deborah? What are *you* doing here?'

Deborah fell into my arms and sobbed for a few moments.

'I thought I would never be found,' she said.

'When did you arrive here?' I asked.

'I don't know. It feels like days ago,' Deborah cried. 'Something dragged me from my bed. I screamed but no-one heard me. Then I was taken through the wardrobe, just as Hilary had been.'

The girl was wearing a thin nightgown and she shivered with cold. Pepper removed his jacket in true gentlemanly fashion, and I helped her put it on.

'Have you seen anyone else?' I said. 'Mrs Lavender was taken. We followed her here.'

'No,' Deborah said. 'Not even Hilary. And I thought she would be here …'

I didn't mention that Hilary had apparently been a runaway and was really at home with her parents. Though I still doubted the story Mrs Lavender had told me on that score, and I wasn't sure at all that the girl would ever return to Haven Lee.

'Come on,' I said. 'We are getting you out of here.'

'Thank you,' said Deborah, and I wiped the tears from her cheeks before taking her hand and helping her to stand.

In the meantime, Pepper and Martin checked the final cage, which turned out to be empty, and they searched the chamber for any other doors. They found one large solid wooden door. Martin tried to pick the lock, but to no avail. It wasn't often that he was defeated in this way.

'It doesn't work the way our locks do. Every time I think I have it, it relocks itself,' Martin said.

'Leave it for now,' Pepper said. 'We need to get this young girl back to safety.'

I led Deborah towards the door, then waited as my companions filled their ears with torn cloth. However, when we passed through to the large chamber, we discovered that the chanting had stopped.

As we reached the first step, I heard a tremendous roar echo behind us. It was coming not from the prison chamber, but from somewhere else.

'It's coming!' cried Deborah.

'Pepper. Take Deborah back up the steps. Martin and I will slow it down.'

'I'm not leaving you,' said Pepper.

I flashed my fangs at him as I smiled. 'Silly. I'm fully ready for this fight. Deborah needs you now.'

Pepper raised an eyebrow, then took Deborah's arm and began the ascent up the steps without further comment. Though I suspected he would give me a hard time for it later.

I turned to Martin and noted he was holding his favourite firearm. This was also one of his own creations, and it expelled fire from a small canister that he wore under his jacket. The barrel of the weapon was strapped to his arm and linked to the canister via a pipe. Gas was fed into the barrel and operated like gaslight, only with a far more powerful surge of flame and heat.

The canister was operated by clockwork. I checked to make sure that the mechanism was fully wound, and then we both turned to face whatever was coming.

'Get out of here,' he said. 'This will hold it off.'

I shook my head. This was one fight I didn't plan on missing. I wanted to see who or what was kidnapping the girls. It was time to solve this mystery.

19

We waited. The roaring sound was monstrous, but the creature behind it never materialised. Then I heard yelling coming from the stairway above us. Martin and I turned and rapidly followed on the heels of Pepper and Deborah. We had been tricked! A ruse designed to separate us from our companion.

The steps ran upwards and flowed downwards and then back upwards. The space had become darker again, and for Martin's sake I lit my bracelet. We hurried back up the final steps to the point where we believed the altar would be. When we reached the top, however, we discovered that the portal had been closed to us.

'Did Pepper and Deborah get out?' I said.

'They must have. There is nowhere else to go from here.'

Martin searched, but there was no way to open the portal again from our side.

'What if we just can't see it?' Martin said. 'Like when you passed through the coal hatch.'

I nodded, and pushed my hands against the wall ahead of us, but it was no illusion. The wall was solid.

'Okay. This is a dead end to us now,' I said.

Then, below, we heard that awful roaring sound again.

Adrenaline pumped through me. My fangs ached. I was ready to stand my ground. We turned to face the steps. Down in the dark, a long, thin, snake-like thing slithered into view, followed by another, then another.

'What the devil is that?' Martin said.

I don't think I had ever heard such fear in his voice before. But I was ready to take this enemy on.

A feeling that can only be described as complete madness and fury, filled with a thrilling devilment, rushed into my blood. Martin backed up against the wall, pulling me with him, though I felt no urge to cower from the beastly thing below me. His reaction to it was interesting. Perhaps I had finally discovered what frightened my usually brave companion.

I took a step forward, but Martin gripped my arm, tugging me closer to him. Then I was yanked backwards and off my feet.

After a feeling of weightlessness, I landed, rolled and came to a halt on soft grass.

'That was a close call!' said a familiar voice, and I looked up to see Edward Brewster towering over me.

Martin was on his feet by my side too.

'Are you hurt?' he asked.

'No. Are you?'

Martin shook his head, but his face was blanched white.

'Help me up,' I said, pretending not to notice his terror.

I stretched out my hand and Martin took it.

We were in Dalentarth, and it was night. The magical forest around us glowed as a pure moon cast down a beam to illuminate the trees around us. The moss-covered wood glowed with silver light. It was a stark contrast to the dark anti-world that we had just been pulled from.

'You must be Mr Brewster,' Martin said. He was fast recovering his equilibrium.

'Yes, indeed. And you two must be insane,' Edward said.

I laughed. 'It's good to see you again.'

'Mmmm. It is that. But, what on earth were you doing *there?*'

'It was a rescue mission,' Martin explained. 'Did you by any chance pull two more people through?'

'No. Just you two. I received a warning that you were trapped.

'Who from?' I asked.

Edward smiled. 'Come on, I'll get you back to where you need to be.'

'And how do you know where that is?' Martin asked.

'This way,' said Edward.

Martin and I exchanged a look, then I shrugged. We followed Edward through the forest as a cluster of fireflies danced around us.

There was a small campfire burning in the centre of a clearing, and a makeshift spit was positioned above it with a full chicken roasting as it slowly turned by some means that wasn't apparent. But, I surmised, it was likely to be magic.

'Eat first,' Edward said. 'Get your strength back. You are going to need it.'

'That's kind of you. But we need to hurry back. Pepper and Deborah may be in danger.'

Edward sat down by the fire on a conveniently-placed

log. He motioned towards another log, and Martin and I sat, even though we both knew it was imperative that we got back to our own world and particularly the school. It somehow felt as though we couldn't refuse his hospitality.

'The portal you need isn't ready yet,' said Edward. 'You might as well take a moment and eat.'

It was pointless asking him any questions, as I knew he probably wouldn't answer, and so we accepted his hospitality. As the smell of the cooking poultry reached my nostrils I realised I was hungry.

Edward broke off a chicken leg and passed it to me, and I began to eat it. It was hot and delicious and perfectly cooked. I finished it quickly. Martin did the same with his piece.

'Where were we?' Martin asked. 'And how do you know about that place?'

'What you speculated earlier was correct,' Edward said.

'Meaning?' I asked.

'Your world is in terrible danger. I have been watching changes to it for some time.'

'The two worlds are converging?' Martin said.

Edward nodded. 'All that you suspect to be true, is true.'

'What was that creature?' I asked.

'That was one of the Old Ones. And you were in their world.'

'What do they want?' Martin asked. 'Why are they doing this?'

'It's time for you to return,' said Edward. 'You're ready.'

Excitement coursed through me again at his words. I *was* ready, but now I also felt a little more in control of that insane, somewhat suicidal streak that had emerged earlier when I was about to face the creature on the stairs.

'Do you know anything about that thing?' I asked Edward, not expecting a straight answer.

'It is an ancient God,' Edward said.

'God? It looked like a monster,' I said.

'Who is to say what Gods *should* look like?' Edward smiled.

'It comes from another world, another dimension?' I said.

'I only confirm what you already know.'

'Tell us something we don't know, then,' said Martin. 'Like, how is this possible, and why is it taking the girls?'

'Humans are very foolish creatures. They can be led astray so easily. A little knowledge can be a dangerous thing,' Edward said.

'That sounds like a proverb,' I said. 'Please explain, Edward.'

The fireflies began to buzz around the campfire, and Edward turned as a small swarm of the insects gathered around him. He became still, as though listening.

'Your presence here has been discovered,' Edward said.

'By whom?' I asked.

'The Queen of the Dark Court. She will be angry that I interfered. We must leave now!'

Edward waved a hand over the campfire, and the flames, chicken and spit disappeared. There was no evidence of the fire even being there.

We followed him back the way we had come, until Edward stopped by a large oak tree.

'Is this the same tree from the first time?' I asked.

'Yes,' Edward replied. 'We can go through this time,

as the Old One does not lie in wait for you now. He may not even suspect you will return this way.'

The trunk of the oak opened, Edward slipped inside and Martin and I followed. Then the doorway closed behind us and we found ourselves on the staircase behind the wall that led back into Haven Lee's cellar.

'I'm sorry,' I said. 'I feel that you are going to be in trouble because of us.'

'I am not supposed to interfere,' Edward said. 'But I had to. This ancient evil has to be stopped.'

He reached for the wall, but I caught his hand and stopped him opening the panel, despite the fact that we were in a hurry. I wanted answers first.

'What were you going to tell us before the fireflies came to warn you?'

'This is human interference. Someone must have found a sacred scroll. They are using it, naively believing that the God you saw in the other world will give them power. What they don't realise is that the sacrifices they give mean nothing to this creature – but he will take them anyway, as human suffering is something he enjoys.'

Then, Edward opened the wall with a touch of one finger and the three of us entered the cellar.

Once inside, I hurried to the door. It was unlocked, and why shouldn't it have been? As Edward suspected, our enemy had not anticipated our return this way, so we passed through the room unaccosted.

'What now?' I said.

'Altar room,' said Edward.

'It makes sense,' said Martin. 'We may be able to establish if Pepper and Deborah passed through safely. They might even be waiting for us there.'

Edward said nothing, but he took up the lead, and I

barely had time to consider how he knew the way.

We passed the staircase to the kitchen, and the wine cellar, and moved through the coal storage room. The hatch was still open. It was daylight, but still early morning: a stark contrast to Dalentarth time. As we approached the altar room, that dreadful chanting music started again upstairs. Edward reached the door just as Pepper opened it from the other side and came running through with Deborah.

'Thank god!' I said.

'How did you get out ahead of us?' asked Pepper.

I glanced over his shoulder as the portal behind them closed.

'That's easy,' answered Edward. 'I brought them through at a time a few seconds before you.'

'*Time travel?*' Martin mused. 'I wouldn't have believed it possible.'

'Anything is possible when you know how to pass through to other places and dimensions,' Edward said.

'This is Edward Brewster,' I said, making the introductions. 'George Pepper.'

The men shook hands, though it appeared to be an awkward process for Edward. Perhaps this was not something Fae did when they greeted each other.

'Who's this?' Edward asked, frowning at Deborah.

'One of my students,' I said. 'She was locked up in the dungeon down there.'

'Let's get out of here and back upstairs,' Martin said.

'Not with her,' Edward said. 'She has to go back. She can't stay here.'

'What are you talking about?' I asked. 'We can't send this child back down to that … place.'

'This isn't a child …' Edward said.

We turned to Deborah. The girl looked nervous, and

she kept her distance from Edward.

'You see, this is the problem,' Edward said. 'Someone must have let it out in the first place.'

'Spit it out man, what are you saying?' asked Pepper.

'It's a toy. A thing … from the ancient world. But, I don't know how it got here.'

'A toy? This is just …' I stopped talking. But of course. Why hadn't I noticed it?

'He's right,' I said. 'Her being down there just doesn't add up. And it was Deborah that told me Hilary had been taken, she that left me drawings to point to the creature we saw below.'

Deborah smiled, revealing a mouthful of razor-sharp, black-fungus-covered teeth. No, this wasn't a child at all. It was something else entirely. She was another form of demon. The Darkness had disguised them in children before. Why hadn't I realised?

'The Darkness …' I said.

'The Old Ones,' Edward corrected. 'Leave! I'll push it back to the portal.'

'You can't do this alone!' I said and I retrieved my dagger and pointed it at the Deborah-thing. The creature's smile widened as its skin tones changed. Gone was the pink flush of youth, replaced by the sallow and wrinkled skin of an old hag.

Deborah-thing laughed. She had the cackle to suit the face. She shrugged away Pepper's jacket, and her nightdress changed, turning into a red robe of the kind the worshippers had worn the night before. The face altered. Elongated. And snake-like appendages grew from under her nose, covering her mouth. They flowed like octopus tentacles in water. It was the ugliest, most monstrous sight I had ever seen.

'Where is Mrs Lavender?' I asked her.

A new surge of adrenaline coursed through me, my fangs revealed themselves and I hissed at her. The creature leapt back in fright. The sight of my fangs was clearly intimidating, though the knife should have been more so, because my oral daggers were tiny in comparison.

I advanced on her, keeping my fangs exposed, and she shrank back towards the altar room, then turned and ran, opening the portal with the speed of practice. The altar disappeared, the steps reappeared, and then the creature plummeted through the portal. The altar reformed as though it had never disappeared in the first place.

20

'We have to get this open again,' I said. 'Mrs Lavender is still down there. That creature was there to distract us.'

Martin moved to reopen the portal, but this time it didn't work.

'She's blocked the way,' I said. 'Edward, what can we do? Can we go back in the way you pulled us out?'

Edward was frowning. 'Things are worse than I feared.'

'In what way?' Martin asked.

'I thought this was humans dabbling with an ancient text that they didn't understand. I had wondered where they found the text in the first place, but this is ...'

'Tell us,' I said.

'I think Fae are behind it.'

'But why?' I said. 'What would they gain from this?'

'The Dark Sidhe are a world unto themselves,' Edward said. 'Who knows what the Unseelie Queen plans?'

'The Dark Court, you mean?' said Martin. 'I have been doing research on the subject, though obviously all I can find are fairytales.'

'The Tuatha Dé Danaan are the originators of such

tales,' Edward explained, 'but man creates its own myths around us. Cerydis is our current queen, though fiction will never report her name. I suspect you are the first humans to ever hear it.

'You know already that the Unseelie were made as a game by a wayward Seelie King. They remained captive until Cerydis was crowned. She took the initiative to form a truce along with the Queen of Light, Aleora, who had sympathised with the Dark Sidhe's plight and was happy to form the truce. Though we are still at odds with them, we have lived in a kind of peace in recent years.'

'You said … Cerydis is *your* current queen. Are you from the Dark Court, then?' I asked.

'Yes. But … I try to avoid the politics of either court.'

'Forgive me for saying this, but you don't look monstrous …' I pointed out.

Edward smiled. 'My appearance is whatever I want it to be. I can be what humans consider monstrous.'

'This is merely a façade?' I asked.

Edward smiled again, and I left it there. Did I really want to see what his real appearance was? Probably not.

'It sounds as though everything in your world is perfect now. Why would Cerydis spoil that and send her creatures here?' asked Martin.

'I don't know. But we can look into the world there, and see …' Edward said.

He turned and faced the wall by the door, then, raising a hand, he illuminated the wall. The wall shimmered, became transparent. It was as though we were looking into a pool of water that rippled and then became smooth. A series of images flashed before us. We saw the Unseelie Queen, with her long, flowing black hair, kneeling before the Seelie Queen, who had silver white locks.

Sound came from the image, and I experienced a sense

that we were in the room, really watching the proceedings.

'Cerydis, Queen of the Dark Fae, do you accept our terms?' asked the white-haired queen.

'Without reserve,' Cerydis said. 'As Queen of the Unseelie Court, I pledge allegiance to you, Aleora, Queen of the Seelie Court. Should our treaty be compromised, we accept that the Light Court will imprison us once more. This time with no reprieve.'

'And do you, Edward, King and consort to Cerydis, agree to abide by our treaty?' asked Aleora.

I saw Edward Brewster step forward then. He kneeled before Aleora and gave his promise.

The scene unfolded into a jovial celebration, where Dark and Light Fae danced and mingled. There was happiness among both sides and no sign of antagonism. The image faded and we slipped, with some regret, back into our own world, no longer voyeurs of the pleasures of the Fae.

'Cerydis would not do this,' Edward said.

I turned to him, seeing him clearly for the first time. He was a King in his world, and yet he had appeared to me like a harmless traveller. What had he been doing in Dalentarth that day?

'Dalentarth is the forest between our two worlds,' he explained. 'A kind of no man's land where Fae move freely. It is also the place where a seer such as I might go to observe other worlds.'

'You have suspected for some time that someone in your world was involved?' said Martin.

'I didn't know who or what was responsible. I still don't. But that thing couldn't have got out without some help. Now everything points to Fae involvement. But I cannot believe my queen would do this,' Edward said.

'Is there someone who isn't happy about the truce?' I asked.

'Perhaps, but I cannot speak of it until I am certain,' Edward said.

'Okay. Then let's tackle the thing we can for now. Let's go upstairs and find out how Kendal knows about this spell, shall we?' I said.

Edward raised his hand over the altar and muttered something incomprehensible.

'This will slow that creature down if it tries to return,' he said. 'But sadly it won't keep it out forever.'

The four of us passed through the secret panel in the altar room and headed back up the steps. Then we emerged from the corridor again via the stationery cupboard inside Mrs Lavender's office. From the hallway, we could hear the discordant singing in the music room and Kendal's insane playing, which appeared to be growing faster the closer we drew.

We entered the room and found the girls in their choir rows, singing fiercely but each looking exhausted.

Pepper went straight to the side of the harpsichord and closed the lid, forcing Kendal to stop playing.

Edward snatched the music score away before Kendal's hands could reach it. Kendal crumpled over the instrument. His fingers still crooked and twitching.

'I couldn't stop,' he said. 'It was as if the very devil had hold of me …'

'Girls, go to your rooms and lie down,' I ordered.

The students meekly staggered from their rows, some supporting each other as they left the room and headed back to their bedrooms.

Someone had lit a fire in the hearth, and Edward threw the score he had retrieved from the harpsichord into the flames. The parchment was dry and it caught with a whoosh, burning to ash in seconds.

'No!' cried Martin. 'I wanted to see that!'

'Why?' asked Edward. 'It would only have endangered you. It would have gripped you and used you in the same way it has used this man here.'

'Kendal? Who gave you this?' asked Pepper.

'I … don't recall …' said Kendal.

I attended to Mr Kendal. The man had grown old over the last few days. When I had arrived he had appeared to be middle-aged; now he looked like a man who had long since retired. His hair had greyed and deep lines had established themselves around his eyes and mouth.

'Can you stand? I think you need to rest too,' Pepper said. Then he helped the man up from the stool and led him out of the room.

'So that's it?' I said. 'It's over? All because of a little bit of ancient text?'

'I wish I could say this was over,' Edward said. 'But I'm afraid it isn't. It's only just beginning. There are forces involved here that … I'm not too sure how to deal with.'

'Perhaps we need to bring in the authorities now?' said Martin.

'The only thing we could tell them is that people are missing,' I said. 'I had this discussion with Lavender. No-one will believe that ancient Gods and Fae are involved.'

Pepper returned to us. 'I've just met up with Mrs Harris. She still thinks I'm a doctor. I told her you sent for me because Kendal was unwell. I told her that Mrs Lavender is missing. She's gathering the other teachers together in the library.'

'Okay,' I sighed. 'I have no idea what we are going to say to them, but let's do this.'

'May I suggest something?' Edward said.

'We are always open to suggestions …' Martin said.

'You believe that the teachers formed your robed coven. Kendal was its leader. But I doubt they even recall those rituals. Now you need to get them away from here, and the magical influence that has been placed on the house. Evacuate the school. Fake a fire … anything. Just get everyone out of here. That way we will be free to deal with what's coming, without the fear of innocents being hurt.'

'An excellent plan,' said Martin. 'I know how to make it look as though we have a fire without actually burning the house down.'

The house was empty. Those students whose parents didn't live nearby were being taken to the Willoughby Regent Hotel under the care of Mrs Harris and the butler Sheppard, along with Mrs Finistra, Mr Dupres, Miss Callow and Mrs Doherty. All of them had been relieved when an official excuse to leave had presented itself, and they hadn't ask too many questions. It was as though they had been hoping for this nightmare they were involved in to end. Even if, as Edward said, they weren't really aware of their own involvement, they still felt it on a subconscious level.

For a short time Martin had filled the house with smoke, while Pepper had told everyone he had sent for the fire service – which he hadn't. As soon as the place was cleared out, Martin had used a chemical compound to dissipate the smoke. The place was all ours, and now we could decide, unhindered, what to do.

'Do you think that the teachers will ever recall that they were involved?' I asked Martin as we watched the carriages containing them and their students head away from Haven Lee.

'Probably not. Kendal had the scroll, but he didn't understand what he was using. I doubt that this was an intentional coven, merely one that happened. They were hypnotised, if you like.'

'I wish we could have saved Lavender,' I said. 'It's awful that she will just have disappeared without a trace. Especially after losing her daughter to this thing.'

We went inside the house and to the ballroom. There Edward was drawing a symbol on the ground with salt.

'This is something that will draw our culprit out,' he said. 'If I can find out who the traitor is, then I can put them forward for punishment from the Seelie Court. That could well save the treaty.'

I left him to finish his spell and went into the kitchen to fetch us a platter of food and some drinks. We could be waiting for some time, and we all needed to eat and drink and maintain our stamina.

As I entered the kitchen, however, an explosion rocked the house. The cellar door blew open and smoke poured out into the room.

At first I thought it was Martin's smokescreen gone wrong, but it quickly became apparent that this was something else. Sulphur, and that awful odour of the black fungus, wafted into the room.

I glanced through the smoke, down into the cellar, and then I saw the revolting Deborah-thing climbing the stairs, closely followed by the bulbous, tentacled creature that we had briefly caught sight of below. The creature was too large to fit through, however, and the Deborah-thing hissed something at it in a language that sounded like the grinding of cogs.

I backed away from the broken door, yelling to my companions, who had come running when they heard the explosion.

'That worked rather quickly!' Edward said.

The Deborah-thing came through the doorway, and then we heard a tremendous racket in the cellar. I bared my fangs at the Deborah-thing, but this time she wasn't intimidated.

'The Old One is ripping its way out through the coal cellar,' Edward yelled. 'Try to push it back. We can't let that get out into the street. I'll take care of the toy ...'

Martin had his flame gun ready. Pepper was wielding a sword, and I pulled free my dagger, which I held in one hand, while I unholstered my laser gun and held it in the other.

We hurried outside, just in time to see the coal cellar doors smashed from their hinges. The creature oozed out, forcing its bulk through the narrow gap. Smooth tentacles whipped the air. In the daylight they were a bright green and dripping with slime. As the green goo touched the perfect lawn outside the hatch, the grass blackened, and the black fungus began to spread. I knew then that if this thing escaped, our world would become tainted and change from a lush and green plane to a blackened and desolate landscape.

One of the appendages caught Martin as he hurried forward, flame thrower at the ready, and sent him flying. He fell and lay still, I hoped merely unconscious, but neither Pepper nor I could risk running to his side to check. We didn't have time. We had to prevent this thing from getting out.

Pepper threw a grenade at the hatch. The explosion blew away more of the wood, but barely touched the creature. Of course, if this ancient monster was a God, then it was most likely immortal.

I ducked and dived onto the ground as one of the tentacles swept too close. Then the thing caught hold of me as I struggled to rise. Its limb slithered around me like a snake; grip merciless. It squeezed my waist, forcing the air from my lungs. I slashed at it with the dagger, and sent an arc of laser towards the centre of the mass of tentacles. It lifted me off the ground. I found myself looking down into the hatch, seeing two bright glowing eyes shining with hatred in the cilia of its vile face.

As it raised me higher, my blurring vision detected movement at the front of the house. I looked around and saw, not one, but thousands of cats gathering around the school perimeter. They sat on the grass, on the walls and along the driveway. And they seemed to be waiting.

My fangs burst from my gums in retaliation as the creature tightened its grip. And the sight of my small weapons startled it enough for it to loosen, allowing me to suck in air. I swung the dagger, burying the diamond-covered tip into the tentacle that held me. The beast howled. Good! I could hurt it then. I heard Pepper yelling, and saw his sword flash. It cut through the appendage that held me, and I slipped from the beast's grasp.

The creature retreated into the cellar. Wounded, it limped away. But I wasn't done with it yet. I had to make sure that this thing would never return to the school. Ignoring shouts of warning from Pepper, I leapt down into the cellar after it.

I could hear it moving, a wounded thing, back towards the altar room and the safety of its own realm. Ahead of it I heard the sounds of battle; Edward was pushing the Deborah-thing back too, and this meant he was in between her and the Old One.

'Edward, look out!' I called.

Then the creature stopped moving, Deborah-thing

stopped fighting, and Edward grew still.

Smoke was coming up from the open portal in the altar room as I entered. It looked as if the fires of hell were bursting free into our world.

A figure rose from the smoke, a pale, beautiful vision in regal blue. Long white hair flowed over her shoulders. I recognised the Seelie Queen from the vision that Edward had permitted us to see.

Edward fell to one knee before her.

'Queen Aleora,' he said. 'Forgive me. I was trying to find the guilty party. Please, this is not a conspiracy from the Unseelie Court.'

'Rise, King Edward,' Aleora said. 'You have fought bravely to save your people, and the treaty deserves to stand. But … I'm afraid you have been duped.'

'I don't understand, my Queen,' said Edward.

'Who has the power to raise the Old Gods? Who has access to the scrolls?'

'Why … these things are kept in the Seelie Court.'

Aleora smiled, and it was angelic, beautiful. I almost fell to my knees before her, but the reality of the situation was dawning on me faster than on Edward.

'She did it,' I said.

Edward glanced at me. 'No. And please stay out of this, Kat.'

'Your human toy is right, Edward. Only I could release those scrolls, and I did so, directly into the Kendal human's hands.'

'But why?' asked Edward. 'You might have destroyed this world.'

Aleora laughed. It was like music. Bewitching. My weapons slipped from my fingers, falling to the stone floor with a clatter. I held onto the wall beside me. I could so easily have succumbed to her siren voice, her smile: become her slave.

'I was bored. And how else could I frame Cerydis? How else could I ensure that the treaty was broken? What greater crime could the Unseelie Court commit, but to interfere with humanity?'

'We would never do that!' Edward said.

'Of course you wouldn't,' laughed Aleora. 'But I would.'

'You've killed people. Murdered innocent children in this vendetta. But I don't understand you. Why form a treaty if you intended to break it?' Edward said.

'For sport, King Edward. And your wife, Cerydis, will take all of the blame. She will be expelled from the throne, another will reign in her place ... someone more pliable. And, as her King, you'll be exiled too.'

I was swamped in her perfume. It smelt of summer days, fields of full and blooming flowers. It was heady and sensual. I struggled to concentrate on her words, and then her power waned. Another spell surged in its place as an equally beautiful Fae, with long, dark, shiny hair, appeared via the secret panel. She was the midnight to Aleora's midday. The winter to her summer. Her power was as rich as her beauty.

My free will returned, and with it my urge to destroy the creature that had taken the lives of so many – as I now knew, just for sport.

'Your guilty confession has been heard by the council,' Edward said. 'Behold, my queen, Cerydis, has shown them your crime.'

Aleora turned. She yelped at the sight of Cerydis. Then realised that everything Edward had said was true. She had been found out. Her guilt had been revealed to what must have been some higher authority.

'You!' Aleora yelled. Then she uttered some words of power that burnt my ears, and I collapsed against the wall once more.

The Old One moved. It raised a thick tentacle and snaked it towards Edward, who was thrown hard against the wall. Cerydis yelled, and raising her hand, she sent a stream of dark light towards the creature. It shrivelled, moving frantically back towards the open portal. Then the ancient God fell down onto the stone steps. I knew that it was mortally injured, if not dead.

The portal closed. Aleora was left floating above it.

The Deborah-thing dived at Cerydis, but the creature was no match for the Unseelie Queen, and she crumpled under the force of her dark, crushing beam.

Cerydis hurried to the side of Edward.

'My husband,' she said.

Edward opened his eyes, but the light was dying within them.

'It wasn't her fault ...' Edward said.

'I need to get him back to the court if he is to be saved,' Cerydis said. Then she looked directly at me. 'You're the Cat,' she said. 'You can finish what I cannot.'

Aleora's scream of rage shook me from my daze, and I turned towards her. Once more my fangs were out as I saw her float towards Cerydis and Edward.

'Then he'll die,' Aleora said. 'Like the humans he cares so much about.'

'Take him away,' I said. 'I've got this.'

Aleora looked at me then. Her laughter no longer beguiled me: it now sounded like a cutthroat razor being stropped on a leather strap. And she really wasn't that pretty, not once the glamour slipped and you took a really close look at her.

Cerydis and Edward disappeared.

I addressed Aleora. 'You can start by telling me if Mrs Lavender still lives,' I said.

Aleora threw back her head and laughed harder. When she straightened up again, her face had changed. I was looking at the plain and ordinary Mrs Lavender.

'So. I was duped also,' I said. 'You're a clever little fairy, aren't you? Everything you said, the story of the missing daughter. It was all a lie.'

'Mrs Lavender did exist once,' Aleora said. 'But Kendal used her as a human sacrifice to his ancient God.'

'You made that poor man kill her? Then you took her place?'

Aleora approached me. 'Yes. And all of her memories. Now, I shall enjoy killing King Edward's toy.'

'I'm no-one's toy. And don't underestimate the human race!'

I dived towards her before she could react. And that was when I discovered that I had another new talent: I could move with the speed of a cat.

Aleora fell aside, but I anticipated her reaction and caught hold of her around the waist in much the same way that her creature had captured me. She stopped floating and fell to the ground with me. I did not release my grip, even though she rolled on the floor with me as though I were a flame she was trying to put out. My fingers gripped hard. Nails dug into her skin through her clothing. One good winding deserved another, and that surge of adrenaline came rushing up again, giving me a newfound strength.

Aleora beat at me with her hand. I had no idea why she couldn't use her magic, as I assumed she must have some in equal measure to Cerydis.

Then there was a burst of music. I could feel her attempts to open the altar portal, and perhaps bring back the beast, as she directed her strength through her free hand behind me.

The foundations of the house, already compromised from the attack, shuddered as her strength unleashed. I knew I had to stop her. I crawled up her body, reaching for that hand, then came face to face with her.

She switched on her glamour. I experienced a rush of euphoria, but then my fangs elongated and I found myself hissing through them like a cat. Aleora's glamour dropped at the same time as I tipped my head down and bit through her royal blue dress, deep into her shoulder.

Aleora screamed! I jumped away from her, back on all fours like a cat, as I watched her body roll again. She smashed into the wall near the secret panel, then rolled backwards, crashing into the altar. She clawed at her shoulder, tearing away fabric and flesh as though trying to remove venom. That was when I saw the final change take place.

Like a mask being removed, the Queen of the Seelie court changed. She was no longer beautiful, no longer ethereal. She was as monstrous as the tentacled creature she had summoned, and more so than the Deborah-thing had been. She thrashed and turned, writhed and moaned, but the poison of my bite was coursing through her cold blood, expelling life from every atom.

'She was one of them,' I said. 'Not a Fae, but one of the Old Ones. It was the ultimate disguise.'

Then, the creature just stopped moving.

'Oh my God!' said Pepper from the doorway. I glanced at him and saw that he was holding up Martin.

Martin had a head injury. He was weak, but mobile.

My fangs shrank back. I felt instantly ashamed as I realised that my friends had seen what I had done. I was a vampire, I had bitten what I had thought was the Seelie Queen, I had drunk … No, wait. I had bitten her, but *not* drunk from her.

'I think we now know what type of hybrid you are, Kat,' said Martin.

'I wish you hadn't seen that,' I said.

'I'm glad we did. It explains many things. Why you don't have the vampires' bloodlust, for example. You're a cat. You are your own namesake. When your cat, Holly, healed your wounds, she gave you something of her own abilities.'

'But what about the vampire abilities? Being able to see in the dark, rapid healing?'

'Yes. You have those too. But Holly made sure that you are more cat than vampire,' Pepper explained.

I became aware of my position on the ground, still on all fours, and I unravelled myself from my obviously cat-like pose and stood up.

The body of the Old One was vanishing. Slipping back, I assumed, to its own realm.

The altar opened one last time.

I ventured down the steps with Pepper and Martin by my side. The ancient tentacled creatures were nowhere to be seen as we reached the large chamber and then hurried on to the room containing the cages beyond.

There we found the door we had tried to open previously, now ajar. And, in a small chamber inside the room, we found the *real* Aleora, Queen of the Seelie court. She was frail, thin, had clearly been tortured by the creatures for her knowledge.

As Martin cut through the chains that bound her, the Queen began to fade.

'What's happening?' I asked.

'The Fae are collecting her,' Martin said intuitively, and I knew he was right.

'But I wanted to know. Why her? How did this all happen?' I said.

There were many things left unexplained, but a few days later, Shirley-Anne and two of the other missing girls were returned to Haven Lee by Queen Cerydis. One of them was Mary Cressman, the other was Hilary Morely, the girl who had gone missing on my first night at the school. Now I could look back and see the lies. The Old One had replaced Aleora, and then Mrs Lavender, and the Deborah-thing had been perfectly placed to take the girls whenever she wanted.

The house was still empty but for Pepper, Martin and me when Cerydis arrived. We had wanted to make sure that the crisis really was over before we gave the teachers the all-clear to return.

'Aleora had been using the girls as her own handmaidens,' Cerydis explained. 'They were just human toys to her. The court had accepted her eccentricity, not knowing that really this was an ancient evil that had replaced our Queen. I'm sorry. But the good thing is, these three won't remember anything, we've made sure of that.'

'Thank you,' I said.

'And the man the Old Ones corrupted, Kendal you call him, I believe …'

'Yes?'

'We have restored his vigour, and erased his

memory.'

'Again, I thank you. Before you go, can you tell me this … How is Edward?'

'He died,' Cerydis said. 'But he'll be reborn again. Such is the way of my people.'

'And the real Seelie Queen? How is she now?'

'She is imprisoned,' Cerydis said. 'A successor will be appointed to replace her.'

'But why? Surely she was a victim too?' I said.

'The Queen knew what she was doing when she made a bargain with the Old Ones. They promised her a song that would unmake the Unseelie. Reverse our creation.'

'You would no longer exist?' I said. 'That's horrible! But why did she want that?'

Cerydis shook her head. There was sadness in her dark eyes.

'Light and Dark can never really coexist. All we can do is compromise. Aleora wanted all of the Fae to be under her influence, and that could never be while the Seelie existed. She was foolish to trust the Old Ones, whose main agenda was to gain access to your world. To dominate it. It always has been their ultimate goal.'

I watched the Unseelie Queen fade away, and I was immediately struck with how fortunate we were that she was not as dark as her role and realm suggested.

The Fae wanted peace, especially the Unseelie Court, who had clearly suffered enough. I hoped for their sake that they could achieve it in the light of Aleora's betrayal.

'Pepper,' I said. 'Let's get Shirley-Anne and her friends back to their parents.'

'You bet,' said Pepper.

'Martin?'

'Yes, Kat,' he said and I paused at the sound of my name. The changes in me were something we could continue to explore going forward, but I was just getting used to the thought that I was a hybrid.

'Let's fire up the airship,' I said. 'I've a hankering for home. I bet these girls would enjoy the ride on it too!'

'Definitely,' Martin said.

I led the girls out of Haven Lee and, as we waited on the steps for Martin to bring the ship to us, I noticed that little beige and grey cat that I had spotted on the day I arrived. She was now sitting at the end of the drive, grooming her fur. Somehow I knew that she had been there all along, guarding the driveway, as a last defence. If the monster had got past us, then she and her friends would have joined the fight.

Amber eyes met mine and then, as if she knew what I was thinking, she winked at me.

I blinked, and she was gone.

So fleeting was the contact, but so important and precious.

About The Author

Award winning author Sam Stone began her professional writing career in 2007 when her first novel won the Silver Award for Best Novel with *ForeWord Magazine* Book of the Year Awards. Since then she has gone on to write several novels, three novellas and many short stories. She was the first woman in 31 years to win the British Fantasy Society Award for Best Novel. She also won the award for Best Short Fiction in the same year (2011).

Stone Loves all genus fiction and enjoys mixing horror (her first passion) with a variety of different genres including science fiction, fantasy and Steampunk.

Her works can be found in paperback, audio and eBook.

More Titles By Sam Stone

<u>KAT LIGHTFOOT SERIES</u>
Steampunk, horror, adventure series
1: ZOMBIES AT TIFFANY'S
2: KAT ON A HOT TIN AIRSHIP
3: WHAT'S DEAD PUSSYKAT
4: KAT OF GREEN TENTACLES

<u>JINX CHRONICLES</u>
Hi-tech science fiction fantasy trilogy
1: JINX TOWN
2: JINX MAGIC
3: JINX BOUND (Coming 2016)

<u>THE VAMPIRE GENE SERIES</u>
Horror, fantasy time-travel thrillers
1: KILLING KISS
2: FUTILE FLAME
3: DEMON DANCE
4: HATEFUL HEART
5: SILENT SAND
6: JADED JEWEL (Coming 2016)

THE DARKNESS WITHIN: FINAL CUT
Science fiction horror short novel

ZOMBIES IN NEW YORK
AND OTHER BLOODY JOTTINGS
Thirteen stories of horror and passion. and six
mythological and erotic poems from the pen of the new
Queen of Vampire fiction.

ZOMBIES AT TIFFANY'S

Kat Lightfoot thought that getting a job at the famed Tiffany's store in New York would be the end to her problems ... She has money, new friends, and there's even an inventor working there who develops new weapons from clockwork, and who cuts diamonds with a strange powered light. This is 1862, after all, and such things are the wonder of the age.

But then events take a turn for the worse: men and women wander the streets talking of 'the darkness'; bodies vanish from morgues across town; and random, bloody attacks on innocent people take place in broad daylight.

Soon Kat and her friends are fighting for their lives against a horde of infected people, with only their wits and ingenuity to help them.

A steampunked story of diamonds, chutzpah, death and horror from the blood-drenched pen of Sam Stone.

ISBN 978-1-84583-072-4

KAT ON A HOT TIN AIRSHIP

It is 1865 and the American Civil War has come to an end. Now Kat Lightfoot finds herself in the middle of another kind of war: a family feud involving her brother Henry and his new wife. But what is behind the strange behaviour of this affluent Southern family?

Caught in the crossfire of an implacable spirit's attempt to wreak vengeance on the Pollitt family, Kat must once again enlist the help of journalist George Pepper and the inventor Martin Crewe to find out what really haunts the family's past.

In order to learn what devastating secrets the Pollitts are hiding she must first explore her own feelings for Maggie's brother Orlando, who is one of the seductive Nephilim.

A ghostly steampunked tale of family secrets, voodoo and vengeance from the author of *Zombies at Tiffany's* – to which this book is a sequel.

ISBN 978-1-84583-086-1

WHAT'S DEAD
PUSSYKAT

Nothing ever seems to go Kat Lightfoot's way. If she's not in the middle of battling a plague of gargoyle-like monsters in 1865 New York, she's falling head over heels in love with her friend George Pepper ... which wouldn't be so bad, except that every other female is doing the same.

When Kat is caught in a passionate cinch with Pepper, a wedding is afoot, but no-one expected a gaggle of vampire women to be staying at the Chateau Chantel at the same time ... nor for them to take such an interest in poor Pepper themselves.

Kat has her work cut out ...

A tale of vampires, gargoyles, faith and farce from the author of *Zombies at Tiffany's* and *Kat on a Hot Tin Airship*.

ISBN 978-1-84583-098-4

COMING SOON FROM TELOS PUBLISHING ...

THE VAMPIRE GENE
SERIES

KILLING KISS
The Vampire Gene #1

He's looking for a girl; not just any girl, and dark-haired, brown-eyed Carolyn is the one.

But does Gabriele Caccini, a student at Manchester University, really know what he wants? When a beautiful curvaceous blonde comes into his life he starts to question his motives and emotions; even a seventeenth-century vampire can do that.

Alone in the modern world, limiting his feeds to one a year to avoid detection, Gabriele reflects on the origins of his immortality and questions why it is he who should have the vampire gene, when over four hundred women have not survived his killing kiss ...

But at a house party, a fellow student spikes Gabriele's drink with drugs and his self-indulgent musings are suddenly turned upside down.

FUTILE FLAME
The Vampire Gene #2

A dark and powerful creature threatens Gabriele and Lilly's immortal existence and so Gabriele is forced to turn to Lucrezia, his maker. She reveals to him the horrors of her teenage years in the sixteenth century in the house of the Borgias, and the possessive obsession of her brother, Caesare. Her transformation into a vampire gives her freedom, but leads her on a journey of discovery which shapes the events of the past, the present and the future.

Does Lucrezia's strange past have something to do with Gabriele and Lilly's problems in the present? What is the mysterious entity which seems to be stalking the vampires?

Finding the answers is crucial to their survival.

DEMON DANCE
The Vampire Gene #3

Deep in the bowels of Rhuddlan Castle the ancient vampire Lilly waits, reflecting on the bizarre twists of fate that brought her here.

Leaving behind her lover and maker Gabriele, Lilly treads a path between instinct and survival: always living in fear of paradox. Through a series of mysterious time portals she samples as many ages as she does victims, railing against the forces of destiny to fight her way back to her own time.

From a veritable Garden of Eden, through Viking rape, pillage and massacre, via the Machiavellian salons of sixteenth-century Rome and violent twentieth-century Stockholm nightclubs, she has learned the hard way what being a vampire really means.

Can Lilly now reconcile her love of Gabriele with the freedom she has enjoyed to love elsewhere?

HATEFUL HEART
The Vampire Gene #4

Lilly, Gabriele and Caesare's vampiric life at Rhuddlan Castle is disrupted by the arrival of Amalia: a new vampire created by Lilly's one-time companion, Harry. They learn that Harry is dead, killed by some powerful weapon wielded by a mysterious time-traveller know only as Carduth. Realising that their own lives are now in peril, the quartet begin an incre3dible adventure through time and space. They must track down Carduth, and somehow disable the weapon, before they too succumb to its fatal effect.

Also seeking Carduth are the remnants of the historic order of the Knights Templar who have been tracking a mysterious box for many centuries as they covet the power which rests within.

And all the time, the box is travelling; wending its way through time to seek a deadly revenge on the carriers of the vampire gene.

SILENT SAND
The Vampire Gene #5

Lilly thought that her vampire lair under Rhuddlan Castle in North Wales was safe … until the dangerous fixer Darren Preacher tracked it down.

Gabriele Caccini thought that he knew all about being a vampire, but his life with newly turned lover Anya is sent out of control by the discovery of a new strain of vampirism, one which leaves its victims as ghoulish revenants, shells of the beings they used to be.

And deep in the Nevada desert, Lucy Collins, Gabriele's maker, is undercover, working with the CIA investigating the vampire revenants and what they might mean for humanity.

When Preacher brings Gabriele into the CIA base, Lucy fears her cover may be blown, but there is something far more dangerous than vampires hiding beneath the sands of Nevada … something ancient and vengeful, with an eternal patience and a lust for revenge.

Soon, the ancient vampire family will find themselves facing their greatest foe yet, something primal and insidious, and from which they have no protection …

COMING IN 2016

JADED JEWEL
The Vampire Gene #6